Just another average, life-ruining day.

WeirdEST

Written by
Heather Nuhfer

Illustrations by
Brenda Hickey

A HER UNIVERSE BOOK

ISBN: 978-1-68261-041-1
ISBN (eBook): 978-1-68261-042-8

Her Universe
PRESS

heruniversepress.com

For E.

Chapter One
Least Likely to Succeed

Don't get me wrong, I know that a lot of people would say there are so many worse things to be than completely forgettable, but I would wager that they didn't spend much time at Pearce Middle School. Here the "Ests"—smartest, prettiest, funniest, and fastest, etc.—ruled the school. More than anything in the whole wide world, I wanted an Est title of my own. Specifically, "Artiest," which had opened up at the beginning of the school year and I had been chasing it ever since. This was my dream! This was my destiny! This was—wait, did I hear that correctly?

"Second star to the right and straight on 'til morning!"

I shook my head and brought myself back to reality. Yet again I had been lost in a daydream.

"Uh, Veronica?" Mr. Stephens asked, tapping his red pen on the edge of his overstuffed binder.

I flipped violently through the script as I rushed onto the stage, trying to determine how long I had been stuck in my head. My fingers were stiff from sketching, making me even more clumsy than usual as I searched for the page. The binder slipped out of my hands and fell to the floor with a loud *TWAP!* that stunned the choir teacher into playing the curtain call reprieve of "You Can Fly!"

"Cut, Gladys!" Mr. Stephens shrieked, ending the song with an abrupt jangle of notes.

I clambered across the stage, using my numb digits to scan the pages, not even attempting to stand before I found the right line. Judging by the veins popping out of his fake-tanned skull, I was pretty sure Mr. Stephens was about to succumb to a brain aneurism.

"Uh, but where are we going?" I was so desperate, I made up Wendy's next line. Maybe I'd get extra points for improv skills.

I didn't want to make eye contact with Mr. Stephens. Instead I underlined "right" three times in my copy of the script and stood up as gracefully as my body would allow. Then my stomach let out a grumble that echoed through the entire auditorium.

"Sorry," I whispered.

"You know there are plenty of junior thespians who would jump at the chance to be auditioning right now? To be a part of our distinguished Summer *Theatre* Program?" He added with a flourish.

"I know. I'm so sorry," I said, finally looking up at him. "I really think I'd be great for Wendy. And being at school all summer sounds great. I mean, for theater reasons."

"You are not professional *theatre* material, Ms. McGowan." He narrowed his eyes at me.

I didn't know what to say, but luckily the crisp pop of foam being broken on stage grabbed Mr. Stephens' attention. Jon, our Peter Pan hopeful, had careened into one of the foam window ledges as he tried to "fly" out the wrong window. Mr. Stephens pointed at the door before he put a big smile on his face and walked away from me.

"My dearest Peter, please continue to entertain, enthrall, and exhilarate us!"

Yep. There's the pinnacle of professional theatre.

Everyone else seemed to love Mr. Stephens. He was one of those young teachers who would invite his students over to watch classic movies or have themed parties to celebrate the solar eclipse or the rerelease of an art house movie no one had ever heard of. This was my third play auditioning for his Summer Stock production, but I had never been invited to do anything other than paint sets or make copies of lost scripts. I wasn't sure why, but my gut told me Mr. Stephens didn't like me. It was weird. I didn't feel like he hated me, either. I was just... not cool enough. What *teacher* gets to decide if you're cool enough? That was a job for the Ests.

"They should cast you as Wendy. Or at least let you say a proper line."

"Charlie! How long have you been here?" I whispered back, trying not to disturb rehearsal any more than I already had.

"Long enough to see you in a classic Veronica daze-athon." He chattered away, resting his dirty high tops on the seat in front of him. "Were you daydreaming about Hoth? Were there tauntauns? Did you save Luke Skywalker? That's what I dreamt about last night."

I shook my head. I didn't want to talk about my daydreams or the play. All those hours of hoping and rehearsing Wendy's lines and walking around in a fussy nightgown for nothing! All that practice. Oh, crap. Practice!

"What time is it?" I asked Charlie as I gathered my things and stood up, even though I was fairly sure I knew the answer.

"Last bell's gonna ring any second. Why?" he asked while gingerly picking a loose strand of his red hair off of his jacket.

"Today is the day, Charlie! It's sink or swim! Or, in this case, Volleyball or Spring Formal Club." I made my way toward the backstage as quickly and silently as my flip-flops would allow. I needed to get my backpack.

Charlie grimaced as he followed me. "Ugh. Ugggggh. Not the whole Est thing again, Very, please!"

"Shhh!" I looked around to make sure no one had heard him as I eased open the side stage door. It let out a long *creeeeaaaaak!* that made me grimace, too.

Mr. Stephens turned around, fire in his eyes. He looked at his watch then back at me. Shaking his head he mouthed, "Not professional."

Sliding through the barely-open door, I found myself in almost complete darkness. The stage lights were blotted out by the cardboard likeness of *The Jolly Roger*.

"Someone's gotta knock some sense into that thick head of yours," Charlie hissed, startling me again.

"Geez, Charlie..." I sighed as I felt around for my backpack.

"You looking for this?" Charlie asked, shining his phone's flashlight on my bag, which he was now holding. "See if you can get to your stupid Est quest without your gear."

I reached for it, but he hoisted it well above my head, like his inner third grader commanded him to do.

Annoyance rose up in me, but I squashed it down. Letting Charlie get to me wasn't a quality an Est would espouse.

Instead, I looked him dead in the eye. "I will be an Est whether you like it or not."

Charlie closed his mouth. I was quite proud of myself for shutting Charlie up. That was a rare, beautiful, mythic thing, much like a unicorn. His silence was to be cherished. Not that it would last long.

I grabbed my bag, but, in my gloat-laden haste, used too much backswing. It flew out of my hands, through the curtain, and crashed into Captain Hook's ship. *The Jolly Roger* teetered for a moment before falling toward the stage, the booming thud of cardboard hitting wood joined with the overly-dramatic shrieks of the drama club wannabes as they scurried for cover. The spotlight hit Charlie and me before we could make a run for it. In the midst of the dusty air, Mr. Stephens stood, agape.

"Sorry! Again..." I managed to squeak out.

Mr. Stephens' mouth was forming words, but no sound was coming out. I stared at him, quite aware that he might call on his Shakespeare-lovin' lackeys to bury me under the floorboards.

BRRRIIIINGG!

The bell! I needed to be at volleyball. Now!

Still unable to speak, Mr. Stephens stretched out a clawed hand and pointed toward the auditorium exit. Being the smart kid I am, I ran toward it and Charlie followed.

In the hall, I could tell Charlie was ready to chide me more about the Est activities of the day. We had been through this before. Many times before, actually. Charlie hated the Ests. He thought they were snobs, or jerks, or stupid, or... you know, any negative word you would want to shove in there. He was lucky; he didn't want to belong. Charlie was exactly what he was and couldn't be happier about it. He wanted to wear torn jeans and gigantic headphones, so he did. He wanted to speak with a fake British accent, so he did. Everyone knew who Charlie was. Good or bad, he didn't care. No one would notice me even if I had a unicorn horn spiraling out of my forehead.

I was set on becoming something. Someone. An Est. Artiest was my goal, but I knew I couldn't limit myself. Honestly, I had tried everything—and I mean *everything*—over the past year to make myself one of them. From Future Bankers Club to the Hug-A-Tree Co-op, I'd failed miserably at each attempt. Today was it. It had to be. I only had two more activities to join that might bring out my inner awesome. Making the volleyball team was a long shot, and a sad Plan B if there ever was one, but I would leave no stone unturned. You know, "beggars can't be choosers" and all that crap. After tryouts I would hopefully get into the Est hive: the Spring Formal Club, or SFC as they called it. Every single member was an Est and I knew if I could get in, I would become one, too. Word on the street was that they needed someone to take on decorations. This, my friends, would be the swiftest path to Artiest if there ever was one!

But first, volleyball. (AKA Sportiest.)

I changed as fast as I could. Keesha (Fastest) was running tryouts, and I was hoping to get in early and avoid the peeping eyes of any of Keesha's Est friends who might stop to watch the new recruits before SFC. It was too risky. I knew I wasn't *that* good at volleyball, and any mess-up could affect my SFC chances. Obviously, I would want the Ests around after I made the team, so we could become instant best friends, braid each other's hair, coordinate tomorrow's outfits, and all that.

There were about ten other girls ahead of me, each rotating into the team and showing their stuff before Keesha could send them out and mark something on her clipboard.

I took a moment to breathe and tried to envision myself victorious. That's what all the books said to do. Success was as easy as believing it. *Believe, Very. Believe!*

I was up, and in place to serve. That was good. It was the only thing I knew how to do fairly well. I lobbed the ball over the net with ease just in time to spot Kate (Smartest) walk into the gym and sidle up to Keesha. Was she watching? Nope. They were giggling now, and not even looking at us! I hustled, determined to get their attention. I hit the ball and let out a loud "Ha!" as it sailed over the net. No reaction from the Ests? A new player rotated in on the other side and my heart sank.

It was Betsy Monroe, more recently known as "Betsy the Bulldozer." She had been the Queen of Arts our whole lives, and she never let me forget it. A reign of terror. It didn't matter if it was the county fair blue ribbon two years ago, or a gold star for stick figures in kindergarten, Betsy always won first prize and wasted no time telling everyone about my losses. I typically managed second or third or—the kiss of creative death—"Honorable Mention."

This past year she had taken to photography, which had afforded me a *slight* break from the constant torture. She had been an Est (Artiest, of course) until they unceremoniously dumped her from Est status when she came back to school this past year with about fifty extra pounds, and a new Goth style.

It was Betsy's demise that had inspired me finally to go after an Est of my own. With Artiest up for grabs, my chances were good. Trouble was, Betsy had managed to knock me out of every artistic Est situation, hence my focus on every other possible activity in the entire universe. Now that she had no friends and no life, she had plenty of time to sabotage mine.

I did everything I could to avoid Betsy at school, but right now I was trapped. The only salvation was to make an amazing play that both Keesha and Kate would notice and applaud me before announcing that I automatically made the team, and had fantastic hair. Simple, right?

I got into position, waiting to spike the ball and earn my point/spot on the team, but I could feel Betsy's stare drilling a hole into my head. I couldn't look; it would throw me off my game. *Eyes on the prize, McGowan.* The ball sailed through the air, right toward Betsy—this was it. She would use her giant ham hands to send it back over the net. Then, I'd be in a perfect position to spike.

I was so afraid to look directly at Betsy that I didn't notice that *she* spiked the ball, and it was headed for my face at about eight thousand miles per hour! Frozen with fear, there was nothing I could do...

"Oww!" I screamed in a muffled, yet surprisingly shrill, voice as the volleyball inverted my nose.

I heard someone squeal, "O.M.G!" but I'd lost all sense of normal time and space. It was as if everything slowed down. Did anyone see? Then I thought how silly it was to think no one would notice me getting pegged by the volleyball, which was literally the one thing everyone *had* to keep an eye on. It was pretty much impossible not to notice it breaking my face. Then I tried to act like nothing had happened, to save myself some embarrassment, but it was too late. I was falling to my knees. (See, I told you it felt like time had slowed down.)

From my new favorite place on the floor, I felt the sides of my nose. There was some warmth, some liquid, but it didn't feel... crunchy. I had broken my nose a few years ago when Charlie creeped me out at a playground and I fell down the fireman's pole (don't ask); my sniffer certainly felt crunchy then. I peeked out from between my fingers. The other girls had formed a circle around me. Some of them were covering their own noses while others looked bored, whispered to their friends, or outright giggled. Teenagers, man. I saw a bright flash of light—a camera phone! No!

"I'm fine. I'm totally fine," I lied as I stood up, still cradling my nose. Betsy, of course, was watching from the other side of the net. Motionless. Emotionless. Part of me wondered if this would incite a bloodlust inside of her. Maybe the sight of fresh blood would tip her into a feeding frenzy. Kate and Keesha were keeping an arm's distance, too.

It wasn't until I moved my hands from my nose that the blood really started to flow. As my dad often says,

"The head bleeds a whole freaking lot." A small pool quickly formed at my feet as I tried to pinch my nostrils shut. What I wouldn't have given to be invisible at that moment.

Various shrieks, "eeew"s, and snarky comments rang in my ears as another camera flashed. Keesha handed me a towel with the tiniest tips of her fingers as I stumbled off the court, leaving a trail of bloody sneaker prints in my wake.

The nurse got the bleeding to stop pretty quickly and assured me it wasn't broken. I tried to explain that I already knew that, but I guess describing your nose as "not crunchy" doesn't hold a lot of meaning in the medical community.

When I got back to the gym, the janitor was just finishing up. He had nothing short of a hazmat protocol to clean up my little bloody mess. There was even a yellow barrier tape like cops use to demark a murder scene. For real? If everyone wasn't grossed out or traumatized before, they certainly were now. I scanned the room. Such was my Est mania that I needed to know for sure what Keesha had decided.

"Hey... you?" Keesha said, spotting me. "I thought you'd be with the nurse?"

"Oh, I'm fine. Totally fine," I lied, trying not to touch the giant wad of gauze taped to my nose. "I just, uh, wondered what you thought about my tryout?"

The instant the words left my mouth, I realized how wrong and stupid they were and how crazy I must have seemed. I imagined reaching out into the air and grabbing the whole sentence, stuffing it in my mouth, and swallowing it before anyone could hear it. Unfortunately, more words were already flowing. I couldn't stop the idiotic dribble.

"I mean, if my face hadn't been there, I would have hit it." I felt my cheeks rise up; I was smiling like a freak.

Keesha gave me an unsure look. "Well, yeah," she admitted, "but your face *was* there."

"But if it wasn't?" I asked, silently cursing my mouth. *Why are you saying such stupid things, mouth?*

"Then you probably would have hit it?" She shrugged.

I nodded in complete agreement.

"But, the other players had more plays... and less blood. Sorry," Keesha said, looking back at her clipboard.

Defeated again. I was humiliated enough that I just wanted to leave as soon as possible.

"Oh, no. I totally understand. It's cool. It's cool," I said, slowly backing away like Keesha was a grizzly bear, but worse. A grizzly bear with nunchucks?

I didn't turn away from her until I was about halfway out of the gym. Smooooooth. Ugh. I counted my lucky stars that the gym was almost empty. Fewer witnesses to my patheticness.

Well, that was that. I put my head in my hands and did my best to suck it up. Sure, I was humiliated, but there was one more shot at redemption. Only one activity to go, and I had to nail it. Like, seriously had to nail it or my whole middle school existence would be completely worthless. This was the end of eighth grade. I had to leave my mark. No pressure. Yeah, right.

In the bathroom I carefully picked the tape off the bandage and finally got to see the damage to my nose. Yuck. I washed my face and tried to get the crusty blood out of my hairline. My nose was still swollen and red, but at least it wasn't bleeding anymore. I needed to hurry—I had things to do. I changed back into my jeans and favorite striped shirt. I stepped back from the mirror, taking a moment to really look at myself. Swollen nose aside, there wasn't much of note. My ashy blonde hair lacked the sunny highlights of the popular girls and seemed to grow outward in a poof before it made its way down my shoulders. It wasn't horrible—it just wasn't good. Same went for my height, which was boringly average. I wasn't cute and tiny or gloriously Amazonian. I sucked in my belly to see if I could force some curves. I had the extra padding; it just needed to shift to the right areas. Baby fat or bust, it was time to go. I left the bathroom to find Charlie waiting for me, like always.

"Don't even ask," I said covering my nose with my hand.

Charlie held up his phone. It had a series of pictures of yours truly in various stages of writhing on the gym floor. "There are some good ones. But a lot of them have this weird light thingy where it's hard to see your face."

"What?" I cried as I grabbed his phone.

"Betsy," Charlie answered. "Turns out she is as good with a camera phone as she is with an actual camera.

Look at that definition. That composition!" he joked. "But I'd imagine she doesn't have *everyone's* number."

"Social media? Noo!" I punched at the apps on Charlie's phone. The picture was everywhere. Charlie was trying to stifle a laugh, and I wanted to smack him upside the head. "It's not funny, Charlie!"

He straightened his face. "It's not. It's not," he agreed. "But it kinda is."

I took a deep breath and tried to compose myself. This was all fixable. It really really was/had to be. There was still SFC, the light at the end of my dark, dreary, almost-broken-nose tunnel. I hadn't thought too much about what I'd do if I didn't make SFC, and I didn't want to. There are a few undesirable Ests, let's make that abundantly clear. No one wants to be a bad Est. I'd rather be invisible.

"Sooo, how'd it go other than the botched nose?" he asked as he flung open his locker. Crumpled papers, candy wrappers, and last week's aced history test showered down onto the linoleum.

"Really?" I sighed. "Yep. I'm a loser. Confirmed. Again. For the eleventh time."

Charlie waggled his finger at me like an old-timey school marm. "You listen here, missy—there are better things in this world than a stupid middle school play or volleyball or..."

"Or?" I asked, even though I knew the answer already.

He let out a deep, exaggerated boy sigh. "Or some psychopathic, sycophantic mission to make yourself one of *them*."

I chortled a bit louder than intended. "Excuse me? I am trying to do something with my life. I'm trying to be somebody."

"An Est isn't a 'somebody,' Very. It's the big-*est* waste-*est* o' time-*est*. Made for people whose lives peak before they hit twenty. Who bloody cares?" he said as he forced his locker shut.

"Waste of time? Whaaaa? But look at the perks I've already gotten." I laughed as I showed off my nose. Luckily, my joke made an end to the conversation we had *way* too often.

"You're coming to the mall, right? Ted is working today." Charlie's wide grin covered most of his face.

I looked at my sneakers. Maybe, just this once, he wouldn't pry. "Ah, nope. I still got things to do."

Oh, yeah. I had forgotten that I was talking to Charlie. Fat chance.

Cue the epic Charlie eye roll. "Like what? Come on. The mall has it all. You can draw the amusing and confusing patrons. Like that lady who wears the pink sweatpants and loafers every day. You love her!"

I crinkled my nose. It gave Charlie the answer he didn't want.

"Really?" He sighed again, shaking his head in disgust.

I turned back down the hall. "Last-ditch effort!"

Behind me I heard Charlie grumble, "But it's the bloomin' dance committee, Very!"

~

The Spring Formal Club meeting was about to begin. Before I went inside, I peeked through the tiny window in the door. There they were. All of those pretty pretty people. I needed to make myself go in. *Go. Now, Veronica.*

Something Charlie had said a few days back popped into my head: "Next year we're just going to be back on the bottom of the pile anyway, Very. We'll be lowly high school freshmen. You're in a fuss for nothing."

Maybe he was right, but maybe not. I needed to prove I could be something *now*. This was my last chance before I tucked in to four more years of wallflowerdom in high school.

I straightened all the raggedy, loose pages in my sketchbook so they looked tidy. Being prepared is important when you want something (or so my dad always says), so I had sketched out many decoration ideas and themes for the dance. They were pretty cool. Or, at least, I hoped. They had taken a long time to do. Some would say they had taken valuable study time away from my math final. (Again, that would be my dad... once he sees my grade.) But sacrifices must be made to get where you want to go, right?

I took a deep breath and pushed open the creaky door. The room smelled like fancy perfume and fabric softener. I scanned the room, looking for an empty seat. Huzzah! There was an open space right next to Mrs. Krenshaw. I could swoop in and be in the semicircle of awesomeness. I slipped into the seat without anyone noticing—more importantly, without anyone objecting. Time to hone in on the brilliant and meaningful conversation already in progress....

"Like, gross. I don't want to be in charge of food again. All that guacamole! Nuh-uh!" Hun Su squealed.

Here it was: an opening. The right words said right at this very moment could change the course of the day. Nay, my entire life! I had to be picky, though, and say the exact perfect words. Nail it like a laser beam. Like a snack-loving, guacamole-toting heroine.

"Uh, I'd be happy to head up food and decorations," I practically whispered. Apparently, it was the best I could do. Ugh.

No one heard me. No one even looked in my direction. In the midst of everyone who was anyone at Pearce Middle, I couldn't get a single glance my way. I was invisible, like always.

Bop-bop-bop!

I looked out the window to see who was tapping. Of course, Charlie was standing there, giving me a thumbs-up. I quickly gave him a thumbs-up in return and looked away.

BOP-BOP-BOP!

The other kids were starting to notice me, and definitely not in a way I wanted.

"Can we help you, Miss McGowan?" asked Mrs. Krenshaw as she peered out from behind *Hawaii on a Dime*. Obviously, she took her duties as the faculty adviser of Spring Formal Club very seriously.

My face grew hot. Why did I wear blush today? I was sure my cheeks were as red as my nose now and that thoughts of circus clowns and tiny cars were racing through the heads of my peers.

"Uh, no. No. Just waiting to sign up," I said, ignoring Charlie, who was now bouncing up and down outside trying to get a better look.

"Wait, what? Sign up?" Derek guffawed. He finally looked at me. His eyes went wide when he saw my swollen nose.

"Yes?"

Derek glanced at his friends like I was bananas. "Ah, you're only a fifth grader."

I looked behind me. No one there. Hmm. Oh, crap! He was talking to me.

"I'm—I'm not in fifth grade," I stammered.

"So, you aren't here for detention with Mrs. Krenshaw?" Jenny asked. She looked confused.

Almost as confused as me. "No. I'm here to join SFC. I'm in eighth grade... with you guys."

Derek stared at me suspiciously. "Nah. I've, like, never seen you before. There's no way you're in *our* grade."

"I have two classes with you," I mumbled.

Kate rolled her eyes at her friends. "Derek, she was just at summer volleyball tryouts. It's Vanessa!"

"Oh, yeah, but my name—"

Jenny cut me off. "Sorry, Vanessa, this is an Est-only club. I thought *everyone* knew that."

It was the way she said "everyone" that really hurt me. Like *I* didn't know because I lived under a rock. Locked in a box. In a cave. In the past.

I hung my head and managed to bonk my already sore nose on the pencil sharpener screwed to the edge of Mrs. Krenshaw's desk. It stung really badly, but I didn't want anyone to know what had happened. Tears filled my eyes, but I held them back. Seconds later, my nose started to throb, and I could feel the blood trickling down. Crackers! I needed to get out of there. Everyone was giggling at me. How could I have thought this was a good idea?

"That's enough, everyone," Mrs. Krenshaw said from behind her book. "Those of you who are *not* officially in the club, please excuse yourselves... And maybe see the nurse."

I rushed toward the door as I discreetly tried to pinch my nose, but plugging my nose meant obstructing my view. Obstructing my view meant not seeing that backpack on the ground. Not seeing that backpack on the ground made me trip and spill all of my dance sketches all over the floor. Spilling all my sketches on the floor made me look like a big friggin' dork. Which, at that point, was something I couldn't argue, which meant I *was* a big friggin' dork.

I gathered up the sketches, still trying not to cry. The snickers behind me were unbearable! My arms were full of crumpled sketches, so I couldn't pinch my nose. The blood was trickling down, and I saw it *plop* onto the paper. The snickers turned to "Ewww! Gross!" as the door shut behind me.

I jammed all the sketches in the nearest garbage can and ran as fast as I could out the front door of the school. Hopefully, I'd get all the crying out of my system before I caught up with Charlie.

Chapter Two
Home is Where Your Dad Endlessly Pesters You

"Come on, let's go to the mall," Charlie begged for the millionth time. "*At the Pea-er-ercer Malllll, there's always something new for yoooo-oooou!*" he sang the mall's slogan.

I shook my head. "No, today was a total disaster. I need to hide."

"You need a distraction. Forget all about this silly Est stuff, Very. Besides, Ted is working."

"Ted? He's getting weirder and weirder, don't you think?" I asked as we walked down the hill toward my house. Spring had finally sprung in our little town, and everything was lush and green.

"We wouldn't want him any other way," Charlie said, gently shaking the excess water from a bogged-down crocus. "Come on. You'll be sad if you don't get to marvel at his unintentional poetry."

"Oh, I see what's going on. Your parents working from home again?" I asked. That was Charlie's usual reason for finding ridiculous excuses not to go home.

Charlie sighed. "Yeah... more research crap. For doctors, they sure don't spend a lot of time with people..." He trailed off for a second before the light came back to his brown eyes. "...and they get very cross with me on a regular basis, so you know what I'd call them?"

He waited a beat.

"Doctors without patients or patience."

"How long did it take you to come up with that one?" I snorted and then immediately regretted it as pain shot through my tender nose.

"Just now. I know, I'm *amazing*," he bubbled. "Soooo, mall?"

31

"I just want to go home, see my dog and my dad. Forget I was ever born. You know, the usual," I grumbled as I wadded up more paper towels to shove up my nostrils.

"Okay...." Charlie abandoned his grand plan. "Speaking of your dad, there's this band tonight..."

I already knew what Charlie was going to ask.

"I know he'll let you in, he always does," I told him, "but I'll let him know you're going to be there."

Charlie waved good-bye and left me at my front gate. It was funny to think that he was still afraid of my dad. Though, honestly, most people were. My dad used to be in an actual motorcycle gang. Like, seriously. There's this thing in most gangs, I guess, where if you want out of the gang, they have to beat you up really badly. Some friends, right? Anyway, my dad actually went through all that and has become sort of an urban legend for it. They say that after everyone was done wailing on him, he got right up and went out for a steak dinner. Most people take weeks, if not months, to recover from that. Dad got up and went for a steak. He doesn't like to talk about it, but once I did get him to admit it was a true story. Crazy. That was long before I was born, but soon after he had met my mother.

Now he is a dentist. You heard me: A *dentist*. During the day, at least. At night he bounces folks in and out of the local live music venue called Count's. My pop Rik could knock your teeth out one night, then reset them the next morning. A master of pain, some would say, but not me. I actually know him.

As I pushed open the front door, I could see his outline through the stained-glass window. His hair morphed into blue through the pane. I wondered what kind of house my dad would have chosen on his own, wagering it wouldn't have a dove flying through a blue sky on the front door. I had surmised that my mom was a hippie. Dad, on the other hand....

The house smelled amazing. It smelled exactly like Italy, or what I imagined Italy would smell like: garlic and oregano, fresh baked bread, and tomato sauce. Theoretically this concoction could wash away the humiliation of my day. If, in fact, my dad had zero interest in my life. Instead, he is the exact opposite and has the propensity to ask eighty bazillion questions about everything... and ninety bazillion questions if it's something I didn't want to talk about.

"Rock on! Forever!" blared from his beloved record player.

Must have been a decent day at work. Homemade Italian food and Classic Rock.

"Dad?" I called out as I put my school stuff in the closet. He was in the living room watching boxing with the sound muted.

"Yo, kiddo!" my dad shouted over the music as he came back into the kitchen.

I dropped my backpack on the floor and picked up my little white puppy beast, Einstein. Best pup ever. He wagged his nubby Jack Russell tail as he investigated my aching schnoz.

"Hey, Dad. Smells great in here."

"Lasagna!" he bellowed. "Chuck isn't showing up, is he?"

"Nope. No Charlie tonight," I answered.

"Good. I made enough for an army, not for that teenage eating machine," Dad joked. "How was kid prison today?" He held out a spoon for me to taste the sauce, but stopped short when he spotted my nose.

"Holy sh—oot! What happened, Very?" he asked as he got a better look.

"You should see the other guy!" I joked. "Seriously, though. I just became very close, personal friends with a volleyball. We're getting married in the autumn. Save the date, Dad, you have to walk me down the aisle."

"When did it happen?" he asked, giving the bridge of my nose a light poke. "Does it hurt?"

"Ouch! Of course it hurts! I'm not Wonder Woman," I said, swatting his hand away.

"What *time*? Specifically?" he asked. A hint of anger tinged his voice.

"Why?" I asked.

"I just wanna know," he said. "As your worrywart caretaker, it's my duty."

"Dad..." I whined in vain. I could feel the tears welling up again. "After school, okay?"

A few tears made it out. My dad drove me crazy a lot of the time, but he was still pretty great. I trusted him more than anyone. I had to. He was the only family I had.

"Spring Formal Club?" he dared to ask.

I buried my head in his shoulder. He smelled like cigars. "Yes, I was completely rejected. Then I accidentally hit myself in the face and made everyone laugh at me. Classy. I'm a big old failure."

The timer on the stove buzzed. I released him from my pathetic embrace and went to turn off the oven.

He pointed a butter-covered knife at me and nodded knowingly. "Hey, you only fail if you don't try."

That, at least, made me smile. "Where did you read that?"

"I don't know. Pinterest or somethin'." He smiled back. "Crap, right?"

"The mighty words of a soccer mom," I said. "What about you? How much nitrous gas did you use today?"

"On my patients? None." He winked. "My day was good. 'You gotta floss more. See this is what happens when you don't floss. Here are your dentures because you didn't floss.' Same old, same old." My dad handed me plates. "Now you—spill."

"Didn't work out. I just have to try something else. Again."

"Well, we have a whole attic of 'tries,' Very," he said a bit more solemnly than I had anticipated.

I managed to burn myself on the pan. "Yeow! Mother—"

With one look, Dad stopped me dead in mid-swear.

"Hubbard!" I finished strong.

"Are we really gonna go through this swearing thing again, young lady?" He was not amused.

"You swear all the time," I pointed out.

"I earned the right to swear. I'm an adult." He fished around in his brain for a few seconds. "Um... Do as I say, not as I do? My house, my rules? Fill in your own parental wisdom there, but no swearing. Period. It's bad manners for a kid."

"Okay, okay," I agreed, "but as soon as I turn eighteen I'm gonna swear like a sailor."

"As is your right," he said. "Now eat up, matey. I have to go to the club soon."

~

I waited until the rumble of Dad's motorcycle faded into the distance before I climbed the pull-down ladder into the attic. I hadn't been up there all year, but boy, was Dad right. He had stuffed it *full* with my failed attempts at becoming an Est. It was like a mausoleum for dead dreams! Soccer cleats sat next to a dressform and sewing machine. A book on horseback riding propped up a half-built computer. I hadn't been good enough at any of these things. Why was it so hard to be *something*? I just wanted to be cool. More importantly, I wanted everyone to see how cool I was. Being the best at something that everyone admired was surely the best and quickest way to become the girl that *everyone* knew and admired.

I spotted a familiar light-purple box. It wasn't very big, about the size of a doughnut box, and I knew every bit of history that it contained. Something bubbled up inside me. I couldn't tell if it was fear, excitement, or anger. Probably a toxic mixture of all three. I had promised myself I wouldn't look in it ever again. That's why it had been shoved up in the attic over a year ago. But now, I couldn't help myself. I had to look in that box.

I ran my fingers around the bent edges of the photographs taken when I was too young to actually remember the moment. My mom looked so happy in these pictures. Her hair bounced. There was a gleam in her eye. She held little baby me so tightly. So lovingly. I didn't actually remember her, but I knew she had bolted not long after these pictures were taken. Why she left was a big mystery to me. My dad's explanation of "things didn't work out" had never really satisfied. She really seemed to like me in those pictures. So, why hadn't she ever picked up the phone or sent a birthday card?

I bundled the photographs with the same pastel-pink scrunchie that had always held them together. I noticed my mom had the same unruly chunk of wavy hair that I have. My dad calls it a "cowlick," which is about the grossest name I can think of.

"Guess I can't say you never gave me anything, Mom," I said to myself.

"Bzzzzz!" My phone vibrated with an incoming text.

> Charlie:
> Promise you won't freak

Me:
Dad didn't let you in? He said he would.

Charlie:
In. Fine. Not mashed to bits by
his mighty man hands.

Charlie:
Promise me

Me:
Ooookay. What?

Charlie:
Blake's back. Saw him on my way here.

I took a beat to compose myself. There was this feeling...
pain? Panic? Pleasure?

Charlie:
Hello? Did you implode?

Me:
Nah, no biggie. ☺ ☺

Me:
That was a zillion years ago.

Me:
I almost didn't remember who you
were talking about! LOL ☺ ☺ ☺

Me:
☺

Charlie:
....

41

> Charlie:
> I haven't seen the dude in 1 yr & pretty sure I'd have forgotten him if you didn't constantly talk about dad rock camp.

> Charlie:
> Not buying it

> Charlie:
> And that's way too many happy faces for someone who's telling the truth

> Charlie:
> Also, "LOL"? Who are you?!?

> Charlie:
> ☹

> Charlie:
> Emojis on the other foot now, huh?

I flung my phone onto a pile of half-knit sweaters and looked down at my mom box. A drop of blood fell from my nose, splattering on the photo of Mom holding me at my first birthday party. Today was total BS.

My heart raced. Geez. If I died from a rare, tragic, and devastating teenage heart attack, no one would find my body until the morning at the earliest. My dad would be all alone. I looked back at the box in disgust. Mom had forgotten about us. So we should forget about her. Forever this time.

I went to my room and dumped the entire box into the garbage can, then smashed it down with my foot as hard as I could. I wanted to cry and scream and laugh all at the same time. I felt fractured, like there were tiny shards of every conceivable emotion just floating around inside me.

Time for bed. Time for puppy snuggles. Time to forget this day ever happened, because there was no way tomorrow could possibly be worse. I grabbed my sketchbook and tried to concentrate on Blake. Take me away, dream boy!

~

I could see myself standing in Count's, but it wasn't the club, really. It was an amalgamation of the club and this hill my dad used to take me to for picnics. You know how in dreams you feel like things are other things, like your brain tells you, "You're at the club, dingus," but instead you can see a stage on top of a hill? Anyway, there I was, watching myself. I was happy, beautiful even. My hair gleamed in the sunshine and was about a foot longer and blonder, and it certainly wasn't doing that weird right-angle flip thing in the front that it loves to do. Everything was in soft focus, like in a shampoo commercial. I was waiting for someone. Then I saw him.

It was Blake. He had his military school uniform on. Not really my favorite, but on Blake it looked good. Everything looked good. Just like in so many other dreams, Blake not only knew who I was, but he also loved me. Madly. Passionately. I was the *one*.

He embraced me, and suddenly I was back in my body. Yay! Blake leaned in to kiss me. His gray eyes seemed to see nothing but me. We were about to kiss. I could feel his breath, my pulse quickened... our lips met and—

Wocka-Wocka! Wocka-Wocka! Wocka-Wocka!

My comical Fozzie Bear alarm clock did not make me laugh. Instead, I sighed, stuck somewhere between ecstasy and pain. The best dream I had ever had and a freaking Muppet interrupted me. If I kept my eyes closed a little longer, maybe, just maybe I'd slip back into that dream. I had fallen asleep with my sketchbook on my chest. Clutching it, I remembered the dream, and the sketch of Blake and me. *Go back to sleep, Very. Please go back to sleep!* With my eyes tightly shut, I waited. And waited. And waited, refusing to open my eyes until every last shred of hope was lost.

Pupster Einstein did not agree with this plan. Everything was hope and excitement and walks and biscuits! He bounded onto my stomach and knocked the wind out of me.

"Oof!" I cried out, finally opening my eyes. The little pup with his bouncy, black-spotted ears gave me about a million kisses in 1.2 seconds.

"Little dude, little dude! Good morning!" I squeaked out between giggles. "That's enough! Thank you! That's enough! I just had the craziest, bestest dream," I swooned, rubbing the sleep and slobber out of my eyes.

Then my jaw dropped.

This couldn't be real. This couldn't possibly be real!

chapter three
stupidpowers

I pinched my arm. Then I smacked myself in the face. Yep. Nose still hurt like a mother. They were really here. Or I was crazy. Maybe both.

Reaching out, my hand shook. I delicately poked a hot-pink heart that was about six inches away. It smiled at me and bashfully said, "Te-he!"

I jumped back, knocking into one. *POP!* I gasped—I had killed it. I was an imaginary-creature killer! Poor thing. Surprisingly, it just giggled and said, "Oopsie!" before disappearing into thin air.

"They aren't really alive, Einstein," I said, more to reassure myself than him.

Suddenly, Dad knocked on the door. "Rise and shine, buttercup."

"I'm up. I'm up, Dad!" I tried to sound normal as I lunged for the door and locked it. "I'll be down in a minute."

The hearts were cooing and giggling as they glided around the room. I put my finger to my lips, silently shushing them. The doorframe squeaked as dad leaned into it.

"What are you watching in there? It's a bit early for anime, don't you think?"

"Uh, yeah?" I replied. "I'll turn it off in just a second."

"Very? What is that—"

"See ya downstairs, Dad. *Downstairs*! In a minute," I said in a very grown-up tone. I thought.

"Okeydokey?" he replied as his slippers scuttled away on the wood floor.

I looked back at my dog, who was staring at the hearts. One, in particular, he kept bopping with his nose. He obviously wanted to bite it, but was being a good boy. I got an idea. If they didn't feel pain... Heck, they seemed to enjoy it...

"Einstein?" I said. "Get 'em!"

In a matter of seconds, and a few hundred "oopsies" later, Einstein and I had cleared the entire room of hearts. No one would ever know the difference. I hoped. I grabbed my school stuff and changed my clothes. My mind was going a million miles an hour. What in the helloladies just happened? Did it really happen? Maybe I was still asleep? Maybe—wait—*maybe* it was a lucid dream? I had read about them in *National Geographic* a long time ago. A lucid dream is when you can pretty much control what happens in your dream. It's like you're actually there.

"That's gotta be it, right, bud? I'm not going crazy, am I?" Einstein wagged his tail. I took it as a definitive no.

"Very! I'm heading out!" Dad yelled up the stairs.

I was relieved. The last thing I needed at this moment was The Man with a Thousand Questions poking around. "Uh, okay! Have a good day, Dad!" I pasted a big, fake smile on my face when I said it. I wasn't sure why. It wasn't like he could see me or anything. "Love you!"

I heard his heavy boots clomp to the door. "Love you, too, sweetie!"

51

Clomp-clomp-clomp.

Clomp-clomp-clomp-clomp.

Motorcycle engine. *Brrrrr!* Gone.

Phew!

~

Throughout the day, I did a stellar job of convincing myself that this morning's incident was nothing more than a bizarre, lucid dream. To tell the truth, I *did* feel a bit weird, but who wouldn't after thinking their room was filled with living hearts? Slowly but surely, the day went on, like any other boring school day. For once, school reassured me that I was sane and that everything was okay. Fancy that.

But then again, there's always gym class, which was meticulously crafted to weed out and destroy any positive feeling of companionship, skill, or hope.

~

Panic is a funny thing. It can give you an adrenaline rush and save your life, or freeze you in one spot as the wolves rip you limb from limb. I was hoping for the former. I knew Betsy would be looking for me, as always, and the safest place to be was probably out on the track field where there would be many reliable witnesses. The most dangerous place to be was exactly where I stood right then—in the dark back corner of the locker room. I just needed to contain my hair and get out of there before Betsy found me. I could see the truant hair tie way in the back of my locker, peeking out from behind a mini dictionary. I could also hear Betsy coming—the squeak of her combat boots on the linoleum always gave her away. I needed to get out of there. Like, now! I stretched my arm into the locker to grab the hair tie, but couldn't quite reach it. Stretch…. Got it. I raced out of the locker room, brushing by Betsy.

"Where you off to, Keating?" Betsy growled. "Your nose looks better. We'll see how my aim is today." Her eyes were slits darkened with more eyeliner than my dad had let me wear in my entire life.

I said nothing, per my usual don't-engage-crazy-people mantra, and went outside to meet Charlie, who was already on the track.

"What up?" Charlie gave me a puzzled look.

I looked behind me at Betsy as she came out onto the field. "She just called me a Keating."

"And?" Charlie asked. "What does that even mean?"

"He was an art forger a zillion years ago."

"You arty types are so strange..." he said dismissively before pointing at my swollen, red nose. "At least now she has a real reason to pick on you."

True. With my schnoz o' fire, I was prime for the picking on. I could only imagine if she had seen the hearts in my bedroom that morning: first, she'd have stuffed one down my throat, then taken a picture of it for her beloved Photography Club.

"Are you all right?" Charlie interrupted.

"Yeah!" I replied as brightly as I could.

I couldn't tell Charlie about what had happened that morning. Not only because of the insanity part, but I'd also have to preface it with my Blake dream. Not happening. As far as Charlie knew, I had a normal night and didn't give a flying flib about Blake. Charlie wasn't convinced.

"No, something is definitely off with you..." he said.

I shrugged.

Charlie looked at the top of my head. "Did you get new sneakers?"

"Don't you mean 'trainers', Brit boy?" I teased.

"You just seem... shorter or something. I can see the top of your head." He pointed as he spoke. "I can't usually see it."

"Maybe you grew?" I offered.

Before he could reply, a laser stare with a metal whistle caught us.

"McGowan! Weathers!" our P.E. teacher, Mr. Smith, shouted from across the track. "Run!"

Charlie and I looked at each other, unable to contain our excitement. Wait, no. Wrong. It was actually the opposite.

"Why do gym teachers call everyone by their last names?" I wondered out loud. "It's like they're robotic."

Charlie added, "Maybe that's how they keep themselves from becoming too human. If they had any humanity left in them, they wouldn't make us run laps."

My chortle turned into more of a choke. I stopped for a moment, hacking away. Charlie stood next to me, amused by his own humor.

"Not even ten o'clock and I already have you buckled over. If I had a mic, I'd drop it," he gloated.

"*Weathers*!" Mr. Smith screeched. His face was cherry red.

Charlie had that effect on lots of people.

He then flung his arms around lifelessly while lifting his legs up and down.

"Yes, yes. I'm moving."

I regained my composure and stood up straight, only to be checked from the side by Betsy. I grabbed my throbbing arm and tried not to cry out.

"Ha!" Betsy laughed over her shoulder. "Only nineteen more laps, McGowan!"

She sped off, obviously eager to circle the track and *completely* dislodge my shoulder the next time.

Charlie gave Betsy a look of total boredom before he turned back to me.

"See," he said in his most soothing voice, "she used your last name: future gym teacher."

"Let's just go," I said quietly.

Charlie lit up. "Or, we could go tattle. Let's get her in trouble! She deserves it. For. Sure."

"No," I whispered as I started to run again, and Charlie followed.

"What?" he said, completely aghast. He put his hand on my shoulder, stopping me, "We have the perfect opportunity to give her what she deserves. Everyone saw her knock you, Very!" Charlie flailed his arms around crazily, yet again drawing everyone's attention.

I fought back the tears. I was humiliated again and really wanted Charlie to just stop. Now everyone would see me get bullied *and* see me crying. Perfect.

"No, Charlie," I tried to say in a calm tone, but my ugly cry face was on the verge of making an appearance, and the high-pitched whine that went with it. "I just want to hide. I don't want anyone to notice me."

With that, I literally shrank about two inches in an instant. Now the top of my head barely made it to Charlie's chin. His eyes were as big as moons.

"Whaawoo?" was all he could say.

I froze. My brain waves were going supersonic. I just shrank. I just *shrank*. Something was definitely *really* happening. Well, maybe...

"Did you see that?" I asked Charlie, not sure if I wanted to be crazy or right.

"Schmoo... uh... yoooou just zipped down a bit. Yeah, I saw that," he managed.

I closed my eyes tight. The hearts this morning *were* real. I had just shrunk. I wasn't crazy. Crap.

"Considering what just happened, maybe it isn't a biggie, but Betsy is mere moments away," Charlie said, looking over his shoulder.

I saw her coming. Betsy was laughing and joking with another future Roller Derby queen. There was nowhere else to go. I felt myself shrink another inch or two.

"We're going to tell Smith!" Charlie grabbed my arm.

I didn't want anyone to know I was bullied. I didn't want anyone to know I was a shrinking freak. I certainly didn't want anyone to know I was having the weirdest day of my life. Charlie pulled me off the track just as I got a parting blow from Betsy. My arm turned bright red from the hit, and my face was beginning to match. I knew Smith would make a big deal of Betsy pummeling me, and *everyone* in gym class would be watching. What would happen if they all saw me shrink? I really, more than anything, wanted to disappear.

"That's it!" Charlie shouted after Betsy. "I'm taking you down, Bets!"

I saw Charlie spin around, his face went from angry to majorly confused. I waved at him, but he couldn't see me. In fact, as I held my hand in front of my face I realized *I* couldn't see me. I had actually disappeared.

chapter four
Beware: Here Be Dragon Breath!

I found myself in the last refuge there was at Pearce: the science hall girls' bathroom. It was a tiny room with itty-bitty windows. It had become eternally gross after Tracy Rollins backed up the toilet with a tampon (allegedly) and flooded the whole floor. Soon after, Tracy transferred to another school due to teasing (allegedly). I had gotten the scoop from my dad. Tracy's mom was his lawyer.

Anyway, that bathroom now came with a stigma. No one who was anyone would *ever* go in it, which is why I hid there. Not that I could actually be seen by human eyes at this point. I still was freaking invisible! I pulled myself up on the counter and leaned over, trying to see my reflection, but nothing was there. I ran my hands over my face and through my hair. I still *felt* the same. Charlie had texted me nonstop since I disappeared, but I hadn't responded. What do you say? "Sorry! I'm completely see-through right now! I'll text back when I can see my phone again."

I could hear giggling coming toward the bathroom. There was no way girls were coming in here, right? I tiptoed over and pressed my ear to the door. The muffled giggles and whispers were getting really close. I knew that familiar titter as soon as I heard it. The maniacally cheery tones of Jenny (aka Richest, aka Queen Bee).

"I don't see anyone," Jenny said as she pushed the door open. Keesha followed close behind.

Keesha and Jenny leaned over to check for feet in the stalls.

"Like anyone would come in here now. After that weird girl permanently grossed it up," Jenny said.

The Legend of Tracy the Tampon continues.

Jenny opened one of the tiny windows and pointed at it. "Why don't you use those long legs for something other than running?"

"Speaking of 'that weird girl,'" Keesha said as she stretched her arm out the window and felt around in the bushes, "you should have seen her in gym today! Mr. Smith was really freaking out! Apparently, she just took off. The Bulldozer was thrilled."

Were they talking about me? Did they actually know who I was? Holy crackers!

"I don't know who is weirder, Betsy or that girl, whatever her name is. She's so annoying." Jenny checked her reflection and applied more mascara. "I mean, how desperate did she look at the SFC meeting? It was sad."

They *were* talking about me, even though they didn't know my name. Hey! I didn't flood the flibbin' bathroom!

"Well, at least she tried, ya know?" Keesha offered as she finally retrieved what she was looking for—a pack of cigarettes.

Jenny smirked as she took the box from Keesha. "Sweet."

"That is really disgusting," Keesha said.

"Don't be such a stain, Keesh," Jenny ordered as she slipped them in her bag before returning to freshening up her makeup. "I don't do it very often, and besides, I think it looks sexy."

Keesha shook her head, she definitely did not agree. "Well, it doesn't smell sexy."

"Perfume and breath mints," Jenny gawked as she made a wide flourish with her lip-gloss tube.

In an effort to miss Jenny's hand, I stepped back and slid on a wet paper towel. I clunked into the sink next to them and hit the tap, turning it on full blast.

"EEEEEEE!" they squealed.

The sheer decibel level sent me staggering backward, where I smacked into the paper towel dispenser, knocking it off its screws. It clanged to the floor, shooting paper towels into the air.

"Ghost!" Keesha wailed, looking like she might pee herself. Jenny was now shrieking so loudly only dolphins could hear her. She grabbed Keesha and held her in front of her like a human shield as they ran from the bathroom.

I tried to remember the positives: They actually knew who I was... kinda. They may or may not have thought

I was weirder than Betsy. Yes, they *did* know Betsy's proper name, but that was to be expected considering they used to be friends.

Anyway, I needed to calm down. A deep breath or two and maybe I could figure out what the heck I was going to do next. In with the gross bathroom air, out with the crazy air. It felt good, actually. I took another deep breath and stretched my arms out in front of me. Man, I really needed to touch up my nail polish. It took a second, but my brain figured it out. Nail polish! Nails! Hands! I was coming back into view! I hopped off the counter and joyfully watched in the mirror as my body reappeared. Happy dance!

Maybe if I just made it through the rest of the day without anything insane happening, things would go back to normal and Charlie would just forget. It could happen. True, he remembers what he had for lunch on August 2 three years ago, but that doesn't mean he can't forget little things... like an invisible best friend.

~

At last it was time for art class. Also known as my happy place. Charlie was sitting at our usual table, looking rather dazed. He was staring blankly at a huge hunk of clay.

"Hey, dude," I said casually as I sat down. Yep. Nothing to see here. Move along.

He pushed his glasses up the bridge of his nose. "Where were you? You, like, disappeared."

Sheesh. Hit the nail on the head, why dontcha!

"Disappeared? Ha!" I fake-laughed with the best of them. "No. I just had an emergency. A *girl* emergency."

Charlie nodded slowly. True, pulling the Girl Card was a dirty trick, but I felt if there was a day for gender cards, today was it. Guys will not even attempt to question something labeled as a "girl" problem. Babies. All of them.

"It's totally bizarre," Charlie went on. Obviously he was still trying to grasp what he *may have* seen. "I thought I saw you shrink out there!" He dug into his clay.

"That's hilarious!" I laughed. "Let me guess—did you have coffee this morning, Charlie?"

He nodded. Yep. Charlie has had some weird occurrences due to coffee in the past. One involved him being absolutely positive he could taste colors. Caffeine + Charlie = mass confusion. Hooray for coffee!

"I still think we should have gotten Betsy in trouble," he said quietly as he pointed over his shoulder toward the computer stations.

Betsy sat there, totally immersed in photo editing. Camera around her neck, waiting to go take more pictures that would make the student body want to curl up in the fetal position and cry. Except now that she was on yearbook staff, she would have to find more kids smiling, not sad pictures of lost puppies or abandoned shopping carts (as was her specialty) .

"Oh!" said Charlie. "There *is* something I very much wanted to discuss, Very."

He whipped his hand around to point at the bulletin board, and a small hunk of gooey clay flung off his finger and splattered on the board. The sign-up sheet for the student art contest had been posted on the bulletin board!

"So, the contest—" he started.

"Eee!" I squeaked.

"Better hurry. There are only two slots left," Charlie said as he stuck a googly eye to the lump of clay he was working into a monster or maybe a bust of Ronald McDonald. I wasn't sure, but either way I'd tell him it was fantastic.

Then I sat there. Not completely sure why I was hesitating. Being excited for the art contest was, well, exciting. The art contest winners would be announced a day before the dance. That was too late for me to become an Est, let alone enjoy it, if I won (for the first time ever) and manage to become Artiest.

"Yoohoo!" Charlie broke in and gave me a nudge.

I pushed myself up and toward the bulletin board, managing to arrive at exactly the same moment Betsy did. Gah!

I motioned for her to go ahead of me. She could have first dibs. There were still two spots left and I wouldn't have to endure the fear of her lingering behind me while I signed up. Win-win!

She slid past me, and I swear she growled. Charlie, ever vigilant stood up at the table, holding his McMonster as if ready to use it as a goopy grenade should thing go awry.

Seconds later, Betsy turned around with a sly grin plastered to her pasty face. I caught myself smiling back. Maybe she felt bad about earlier? Maybe there was a chance we could put all that competition and general evilness behind us? She loafed her way back to the computer terminal and I smiled all the way up to the sign-up sheet. Until, that is, I saw that Betsy had signed up for BOTH the remaining slots!

"Betsy?" I heard myself shriek. "You can't enter twice!"

"If I'm entering for drawing *and* photography I definitely can."

"Hey! Not cool!" I continued my shriek-fest as a heat started to build up in my gut.

"Oh, boo-hoo!" she chided me. "I'm Veronica and I'm so sad that I suck at everything! Boo-hoo! I don't know what I am! BOO HOO!"

"Quiet down, you two," Mrs. Brannen said, her black bob haircut swooshed as she turned toward us. Our art teacher is a tiny woman who loves realism and classical skill. Before she came to our little town she was an art buyer for a big museum in New York. Neat, right? Anyway, her obsession with clean lines and photorealism didn't lend itself well to my style. Betsy's art on the other hand...

"Betsy signed up for the last two spots in the contest," I explained.

Mrs. Brannen openly rolled her eyes at Betsy. "Why would you do that?"

"I wanted to enter in two categories," Betsy repeated.

She turned her gaze to me. "Okay. Veronica, why did you wait until the last day to sign up?"

"I just... forgot?" I offered.

"Pssh!"

Mrs. Brannen didn't believe me. "You're in here almost every day. Don't give me that."

"Are you going to let her take both spaces?" I asked.

"She played by the rules. There isn't anything I can do." Mrs. Brannen added, "Maybe she'll give up a spot out of the kindness of her heart."

The smuggest smirk of all time slid across Betsy's face. Pretty sure you need to *have* a heart to use its kindness.

I wanted to yell some more, but the rage that was beginning to boil in my belly left me speechless. I was so mad, I was burning up. This was the most Betsy-like move ever!

Finally, I'd had it, and I opened my mouth to tell her a thing or two, but instead of my obscenity-laden diatribe, a ball of fire spewed from my mouth. It bounced off the bulletin board and hit the coat rack where all the smocks and aprons hung, setting them ablaze.

Panic took over the room, but all I could do was slap a hand over my fire-breathing mouth. It had happened again—another crazy moment; except this time, *everyone* could see it. But did they see it had come from me? I didn't think so.

The sprinkler system went off as the whole school was rushed out of the building. I grabbed the loop on Charlie's backpack as we lined up on the lawn. We needed to stay together.

The fire department had arrived. Oh, brother. It was just one tiny little smock fire. No one would even miss them. Turns out, someone had seen my fire breath—Charlie. Oh, crap. Or maybe he was just staring at me for some other reason I was completely unaware of? Then he looked at the smoking school, the firefighters, and back to me.

"It was you?" he said.

"It wasn't me! Why would I set art on fire?"

"It. Was. You!" His eyes were alight.

Wait, what? He seemed... happy?

In a flash, I was swept up by local anchorman Stormy Raines (there's no way that's his actual name, am I right?), who gripped my arm so tightly I thought we'd be bonded forever. The cameraman snapped his fingers and pointed at Stormy, directing him to talk, as he pressed the camera too close to our faces.

Stormy flashed his giant squirrel-toothed smile. "I'm here with a student who saw it all! What's your name, little lady?"

I eked out, "I... I McGowan?"

73

"What did you see? I heard you *eye witnessed* the Molotov cocktail?" Stormy asked me with great mock concern.

"Uh, no. No, I didn't." The cameraman's assistant turned on another light, dazing me even more. "There was just this, like, ball of fire..." I caught myself saying.

"Ha-ha!" Stormy boomed. "Obviously this young girl is shocked to the core! The school has yet to comment, but this reporter feels confident enough to call it a bout of Weird Science from the school lab! Back to you, Chet."

I walked aimlessly away from the hustle and back to Charlie who was still grinning ear to ear.

"So, it was a *ball* of fire?" he asked. "That's seriously the coolest thing I've ever seen."

I was very confused. "You think all of this is cool?"

"Very, my mate, my curmudgeonly gal pal, you can shrink and breathe fire and—and who knows what else?"

"What's wrong with you? This is the worst thing ever!"

Charlie threw his hands in the air. "Are you kidding me? This is like an origin story!"

I rolled my eyes. "An origin story is about a superhero who has useful powers, Charles. *Super*powers, not *stupid*powers. Besides, this is just a—a thing. A one time, one-day deal. They're going to go away."

"How do you know that?"

"Because I do," I said in a tone that would tell any reasonable person to stop pressing.

"Yeah, but *how*?"

"Because they have to go away." I looked around to see if any teachers were nearby. "I need to get out of here."

"And go where? Charles Xavier's School for Mutants?"

Before I could smack the ear-to-ear smile off Charlie's face, Principal Chomers gave the all clear to go back inside. The fire had been contained and extinguished with zero damage to the rest of the school. So, yeah, it was too late; I would have to endure the rest of the day. Luckily there was only one period left. Not-so-lucky that it was to be spent working in the school office.

~

A little trickier, but I thought that more than likely, everyone would be too busy talking about the fire to notice me if something weird were to happen. I was right. The office was chaos. Everyone wanted to know what had happened. I volunteered to answer phones; a brilliant idea, I thought. Lots of parents called to make sure their kid was fine, and I could be busy without anyone seeing me. That was the true beauty of telephonic communication. Every kid was fine. Every single one of them. Well, except for me, but I certainly didn't tell that to any of the concerned parents. I was beginning to get annoyed with their way-too-similar calls until I got one that scared me more than anything.

"Hello, I'm detective, ummm... Mulder calling about the fire earlier today. Has the local PD confirmed a cause yet?" a stern female voice said.

"Uhh, PD? As in Police Department?" I asked.

"Affirmative. As in righty-o," the detective said.

"I know what 'affirmative' means." I caught myself getting annoyed. Who says 'righty-o'? *Zip!* A tiny blue electrical bolt shot from my finger into the phone's mouthpiece.

"Yowch!" the detective exclaimed.

Ahh! I had just zapped an officer of the law.

"I need full names and addresses of all students and faculty who may have seen anything unusual," she demanded.

"Un-unusual, like what?" I stammered.

There was a long pause before the detective asked, "To whom am I speaking?"

"Uh, Veronica..." I said.

"Veronica?" She sounded surprised. "Did you witness the incident?"

Ack! This wasn't good. Evacuate! Evacuate!

"You're b-eak-ing u-p! I-have-to-go-now-bye!"

I clapped down the receiver harder than I should have. The day was almost done. Maybe take a sick day tomorrow, or, you know... forever. I watched the clock tick every last little second until it set me free. I ran to my locker. I wasn't even slightly surprised that Charlie had left me a note, telling me to meet him at his house "For fun!" I was half convinced he already had a business plan drawn up for our own little freak show starring yours truly.

~

Pressing the secret key code, I let myself in through the frosted-glass door. It had taken me a few minutes to find it, as usual. The front of Charlie's cement-walled, ultramodern house was completely flat, and the doors slid open instead of being on hinges. The house was always cold inside, and there were never dirty cereal bowls in the sink. Everything had its place. It was dead silent today except for the muffled sound of Charlie's stereo upstairs. No wonder he had invited me over—his parents weren't home.

"Charlie?" I knocked on his bedroom door as I swung it open. I instantly regretted not waiting to get permission.

Charlie stood up looking embarrassed, giving the vibe that he had been up to something I didn't want to know about.

"Sorry, sorry, sorry," I said, as I covered my eyes with one hand and closed the door with the other.

"Get in here!" he said, pulling my arm and flinging me onto a nearby ottoman.

Charlie's room looked like it was in a different house than his parents'. Maybe even on a different planet. The walls were red and covered in posters of obscure bands even my dad had never heard of. The bed was *never* made, and I wasn't sure what color the carpet was because it was always covered in clothes.

"So?" I said, looking at Charlie.

"As you know," he began, sitting down on what used to be a patio chair, "today was a little boring. I think we can do better."

"Do better? Charlie, I set the school on fire!" I threw a pillow at him.

"Well, you've got this thing, right? This amazing gift—"

"Gift?"

"*Gift.* And I think we should use it. Save the world. Make some money. I don't know. Something. Something cool," he said.

"I can't believe you." I shook my head. "Did you even think about what might happen to me if anyone found out about this? This isn't a cute quirk, like, like dimples or your stupid accent. This could *hurt* people, including me. If anyone knew about this, I'd be made into a lab rat, not an Avenger! Things don't always turn out awesome."

Charlie leaned back, with a straight face for once.

"Yeah. You're right. Obviously, it could be dangerous and scary and more like alien autopsy footage. I get it." He nodded. "Sorry."

"Thank you," I said. "Now if you had just thought about it for five seconds before—"

"Ha-ha. I've been thinking about it since I ditched after fifth period." He stood up and revealed what he had been doing when I interrupted him.

A yellow legal pad had the words "JINX REMOVING" scrawled across the top and a list below.

"We're going to *cure* you!" Charlie said proudly.

I had no words. I hugged him as tightly as I could.

"See, I think about things sometimes," Charlie said as he gasped for air.

I let him go.

"I'm sorry I was a pain," I said.

"No worries. Women." He rolled his eyes. "They get superpowers and are smart enough not to want them. Le sigh."

"Just one thing..." I said. "I'm pretty sure I'm not jinxed. This isn't, like, a voodoo curse."

Charlie nodded knowingly. "It certainly doesn't seem that way, but you never know. Plus, it's the title of a really great Jawbreaker song."

"Well..." I smiled genuinely for the first time that day. "Let's get to work."

chapter five
It's All In Your Head

"One step ahead of ya!" Charlie foraged around on his desk (which was covered in pieces of a model UFO he'd been building since I met him) and unleashed a purple stethoscope that had "WEATHERS" written down the tube in silver Sharpie.

"Ta-da!" he said with a flourish.

I stepped back. "Dude, there's no way I can be examined by your moms!"

Charlie guffawed as he struck a statuesque pose. "I would never let those kooks near you! Doctor Charles Weathers in the house! Not pictured: WebMD."

He listened to my heart and lungs, but everything sounded fine, if he even knew what fine sounded like. Our check of my symptoms online suggested that I was only under the influence of hallucinogenic drugs, or schizophrenic. Considering we could both see my powers (like when I charred part of the art room,) we figured that hippie drugs and mental illness weren't the cause.

"Okay, we've tried the least invasive method. Now, let's try something a little more—"

"Invasive?" I shook my head. "No."

"This will be fun. Trust."

I followed Charlie down the meticulously clean hallway. The walls were lined with family photos. One was of Charlie and me when we went to the zoo a couple years ago. His mom Luisa was stroking Charlie's hair. He stared, panic-stricken, at a person in a sea otter suit. His other mom, Daphne, was holding my hand as I tried to lunge toward the otter to hug it. Boy, things had changed a lot in such a short time. Now I was the big chicken and Charlie was the one hugging otters. Or something like that. You get what I mean.

Charlie and his biological brother, Nick, had been adopted when he was a baby and Nick was six. Daphne is British while Luisa is American. Just an FYI, Charlie's accent didn't exist until we started middle school. In fact, he's never even been to the UK, and Nick doesn't have an accent at all. Unless, when he left for college, he took a cue from Charlie and donned a fake one to impress people at school.

Charlie inched the door open like it might be booby trapped. Whoa. I had never been in his moms' lab before and it was absolutely... whoa. Test tubes, microscopes, a centrifuge and shiny metal tools as far as the eye could see! I went to investigate a massive freezer that was the length of a whole wall.

"Don't open that," Charlie warned. "I opened it once thinking they might have hid some ice cream in there, but it was *definitely not* ice cream."

Charlie directed me to a rolly chair and unveiled a weird-looking helmet that had sort of a cage on top of it. I don't know how to explain it. Hmm... let me see...

After the headgear was sufficiently strapped to my noggin, Charlie fired up the computer attached to it.

"Alright, so this thingamajigger can tell what parts of your brain are currently working," Charlie said, gleefully tapping keys as various bleeps and bloops came from the speakers.

"Y-you don't think it can *read* my mind, do you?" I asked. Now I was getting a little concerned. I couldn't let Charlie know all my thoughts. Or, at the very least, about 76% of them.

We saw something on the screen—a blob. Was it my brain?

"I think we got it!" Charlie shouted. He did a little dance, then wiggled his fingers in my face. "Let's find out what's in your mind, Veronica McGowan!"

No! This contraption was going to show all my secret thoughts. And make me look like more of an idiot than I already did with it on my head. I had to get it off. I reached up to undo the chinstrap.

"Very, what are you doing?"

"I don't like this," I said, closing my eyes as I wrangled with the strap. *Don't think about Blake, Veronica. Don't think about anything!*

I opened my eyes and a light shot out of them. Straight ahead of me, I could see that embarrassing Blake dream being projected *from my eyes* onto the wall.

"What in the heck is that?" Charlie said.

I shut my eyes again, and like flipping off a light switch, the projection was gone.

"Open your eyes," Charlie pleaded.

"No, it shows whatever I'm thinking about," I gasped.

"A bad, made-for-tv movie?"

I tried to think about my dad, my dog, and other "normal things" as I opened my eyes again. Nope. There I was, plucking that really scary, gigantic eyebrow hair that grows right between my eyes!

"Oh, that's unsightly."

I closed my eyes tightly again. "Guess it's not what I'm thinking about. It's what I don't want anyone to know."

"Oh, please," Charlie begged, "just one more. It's only me. Who am I going to tell about your unibrow?"

"No way." I couldn't help but laugh a little, which made it hard to keep my eyes shut. "Can we please just take this off? It's making me way too nervous."

"Okay, okay," Charlie said gently as he helped me remove the contraption.

Once it was safely tucked back into a cupboard, I felt loads better. The panic and nerves had died down. For good measure, I put on my sunglasses until I was sure this whole projecting thing was over.

Well, that was another bust.

"Charlie? You home?" Luisa called from the entryway.

"Yep, Mom! Very and I are doing homework," Charlie called as we scampered out of the lab as quickly as possible and went into the kitchen. We cracked open our books just as Luisa and Daphne walked in.

"Hello, Veronica." Luisa gave me a hug. "Whatever happened to your nose?"

"Oh, just sports," I said, waving it off.

Luisa laughed. "That'll do it every time. What are you two working on?"

I said "biology" at the same time Charlie said, "history."

Luisa and Daphne shared a knowing look.

"Well, that should be an interesting project then," Daphne said and gave me a wink.

Charlie turned bright red. Pretty sure I did, too.

"Did, uh, you hear about what happened at school today?" Charlie asked.

"Yes, it was very peculiar," Daphne said flatly.

"And you weren't worried?"

Luisa gasped. "Of course we were."

"But statistically speaking, the odds of you being hurt were very slim," Daphne said, "and we didn't get a call from the school, so…"

"Or you were just too busy?" Charlie shrugged.

"Charlie," Daphne warned.

It had become a bit tenser than I liked. Time to split.

"Speaking of concern," I said cheerfully, "I better get home."

I said my goodbyes and Charlie walked me out.

"They think you're self-sufficient, Charlie. That's really cool," I pointed out. "My dad texted me 800,000 times after news of the fire broke. He doesn't think I can handle anything."

"Correction: your dad doesn't *want* you to handle anything. He's a giant control-freak of a man."

I nodded. "Can you imagine if he knew about my powers? I'd never be allowed to leave the house again. Which is yet another reason they gotta go."

"But how do you make them happen?" Charlie asked.

"Make? No making. They just happen out of nowhere, uncontrollably."

"Well, that's just rubbish then, isn't it?" he said. "There has to be a trigger."

"Sure, or I'd be shooting out hearts and lightning bolts while I write English papers."

"Hearts?"

I forgot I had kept that part secret for a reason.

"Theoretically," I added. Time to change the subject. Quickly. "Uhhh, so let me see… right before the little fire, Betsy kept me out of the art contest," I continued, "And I shrank in gym class when I felt scared."

"And that made you really, really mad," Charlie added. His face went pink with embarrassment. "Crud. Could I be the trigger? I've been there for all the kerfuffles, haven't I? It could be me!"

Considering Charlie hadn't been in my bedroom the night before, I would wager not. I thought about gym class and how scared I had been of Betsy and how humiliated I had felt to have everyone looking at me. Really, if I was honest, the moment I was most humiliated, I disappeared.

"Charlie, I think I've got it. It isn't you." I couldn't really have been sure, but it was somewhere to start, "If I'm angry, I breathe fire. If I'm scared, I shrink. If I'm humiliated, I disappear. Among, um, other things. Maybe, this is all connected to my emotions?"

"Could be."

"Now what?" I asked.

"Tomorrow we get a second opinion. And a pretzel."

Chapter Six
Heart of Stone

The cheese came out of industrial-sized cans and oozed into the warmer. It looked like a cross between magma and snot. Charlie wolfed down his pretzel, snot cheese and all, and handed me mine. But I was busy looking at some hair product that I'd just bought. It promised to miraculously straighten my hair for days. *Days.*

"Maybe you should just do chunks of hair!" Charlie suggested. "Then you'd have your fuzzy, wavy patches, and, you know, normal hair patches."

I furrowed my brow. "'Normal'? Thanks, pal. I feel a zillion times better now about my crappy hair."

"Just trying to add to the conversation. I've given up convincing you about all that stuff." He threw away his pretzel wrapper while we waited for Ted to finish reloading the cheese.

I looked at Ted. King of Pretzelasaurus. I couldn't remember when he started working there, but it was when I was still little. He had to be in his late thirties by now, maybe forties?

"How much did you tell him?" I whispered. I wasn't too worried about Ted knowing too much, since he'd be hard-pressed to find someone who'd believe him.

Pretzelasaurus had been a favorite since we were kids. I used to get so excited when we saw that animatronic dinosaur with the pretzels clenched in its claws. It seemed so gigantic to me then, towering over me, smelling like warm dough and WD-40. Now that dino seemed small and rickety.

"Sparks, yer face done what that of a cherry sucker," Ted said when he turned back around.

Yep. That's how Ted talked. All the time.

"Your face is rather red, Very," Charlie translated.

"Yeah, I hurt my nose." That was as much of an explanation as I cared to give at the moment.

"Ted, Very wanted to talk to you about something," Charlie went on, eyebrow raised.

As annoyed as I could get with Charlie, I was amazed that he never seemed to judge people. Or, at least, he never judged weird people. Which, I realized, meant that I was judging people as being weird or not weird, which was *actually* a judgment on my part. It's all very confusing, if you think about it.

Ted stretched out his plastic-gloved hand for me to take. I shook my head. He just left his hand there, dangling for a long silent minute. It looked too sad for me not to give in. Like an unreciprocated high five. I always felt bad for those people. Especially when it was me.

Sticky glove touched sweaty palm, and suddenly Ted got a steely look in his eye. I was almost worried. I knew Ted was eccentric, but this was a bit much even from him. My heart started to pound.

"I'm here to tell ya..." Ted leaned in. He was more serious than I had ever seen him. I guessed he was probably more serious than he had ever been in his entire life.

I let out a faint, "What?"

Ted looked at me like he could see my soul. (Or like I had something stuck in my eyelashes.)

Then he *slapped* the top of my hand. His seriousness was replaced by a silly grin.

"Stay in school!" He laughed like a hyena.

"You looked so worried!" chortled Charlie.

"Not funny, guys." I meant it. I readjusted my backpack on my shoulders. "I thought we were here for a reason, Charlie."

"That we are, that we are," he agreed.

I stared at Charlie, who stared expectantly at Ted, who stared right back at him, completely oblivious.

"Um, Charlie?" I said, poking his arm.

Charlie didn't miss a beat. "All right, guess I'll get this rolling, then. Ted, do you notice anything different about Very? Aside from her resemblance to everyone's favorite holiday reindeer, I mean."

Ted gave me a once-over, then squinted to get a better look at something around my head zone.

"She always have two ears?" Ted asked.

"Sure have," I answered. Oh, boy.

He followed up with, "Howdya like Icey Ice?"

I looked at Charlie, who gave me a thumbs-up.

"I-I don't know. I guess I... don't hate it?" I replied.

Maybe it was the events of the past twenty-four hours that made this seem poignant, but I had goose bumps.

"Why would you ask me about ice, Ted? It's spring," I asked warily.

Ted had whirled around; his back to Charlie and me. Charlie was blissfully ignorant of the world of confusion that now rested on my shoulders. Something felt really *weird* about this. Something important. Something like—

"Icee Ice!" Ted whirled around again, holding two frozen cherry Icee drinks from the machine behind him.

Aw, Sheboygan. It took a second, but I laughed. I had let all of this turn me into a nut job.

"Thanks, Ted, but I think we need to get moving," I said.

Charlie looked at me, pained.

"You can have mine," I told him.

Charlie took both Icees and chugged one down, a small stream of red food coloring dripping down of the corners of his mouth. An instant sugar rush later, he was running toward the exit.

"Yeah, man, thanks! See you tomorrow!" Charlie yelled over his shoulder.

I followed, but Ted grabbed my arm before I could get too far.

"Ted, it wasn't funny the first time, and it's not gonna be funny now." I yanked my arm away. "Besides—" I stopped. Ted had a vacant look. His eyes were glazed over and serene. He wasn't angry or joking. It was like he wasn't even there.

"Twelve years is bigger than a world apart. Be cool," he said and turned, putting his back to me. Almost instantly he turned back around, gigantic smile on his face. Ted had returned. "Laters, Lady V!"

I nodded and ran to catch up with Charlie.

"What?" Charlie asked.

"Nothing. Ted is just... so Ted. Whatever that is."

"He's so... Zen?" Charlie wondered. "Yeah. Zen. I think. That's why he's so cool and, you know, emotionally open. It's like he doesn't let his emotions phase him."

A light bulb blinked on over my head. Yes, literally, a tiny light bulb appeared. Thanks, stupidpowers! It danced around a bit until I swatted it away.

"That's it. Be flibbin' cool!"

~

The botanical garden was in full bloom. Cherry trees lined the block-sized park, their pink flowers floating through the air. It was beautiful.

And early. Too freaking early in the morning. I chomped the last of my doughnut and handed Charlie the bag. He could entertain himself with the rest while I tried our next experiment.

I had my dad's noise-canceling headphones ready to go. I had synched up a series of guided-meditation MP3s that would hopefully squelch the madness within. Maybe, just maybe, if I chilled out enough, I'd be able to brush off all these feelings and their stupidpowers.

The soothing Australian accent of a man called Randu filled my ears. He directed me through a series of deep-breathing exercises and attempts to let my thoughts come and go as they please. I started to feel a little zoned out, to be honest. I couldn't feel the breeze anymore, or the grass under me. My limbs felt heavy. Impossibly heavy. This went on for a while. It was nice not to have a desire to move. It was like I could stay in this position, just like this, forever... I was so at peace that—

"ACK! UGH! What is—" I sputtered, thrust out of my Zen state.

Charlie stood in front of me, looking terrified and holding one of his nasty socks in front of my nose.

"Gross! What the heck are you doing?" I cried, pinching my nose.

"Look!" he said, pointing to my crossed legs.

"Oh, fudgebuckets!" I said.

My legs had turned to stone. Apparently my *whole body* had turned to stone when I was deep in meditation. From the neck down, I was a living statue. It really freaked Charlie out, so he'd resorted to giving my system a shock of the foot odor kind. I tried to wiggle my limbs free, but there was no give. This was going to take some time. That was when I noticed Charlie kept looking over his shoulder.

"What?" I asked, suspicious of his very suspicious behavior.

"Um, ah, can you move yet?" he asked, scratching his eyebrow the way he always did when he was nervous.

I could feel my legs now, but they were still grey and immobile.

"Not yet. Why?" Though I had a feeling I really didn't want to know.

"Well," Charlie fake smiled, "it appears Blake is headed this way."

No. No no no no no. I used every ounce of concentration I had to force my legs to move, but it didn't work. At this point, it would take something more mechanical, like a crane, to move me. If I couldn't get up, Blake was going to see how freakish I was!

Naturally, I panicked. "Charlie! What do I do, what do I do?"

Charlie shrugged as he took the headphones off me. "I guess Dream Man needs to learn the truth."

Blake would spot us any minute. In a moment of brilliant yet stupid inspiration, I came up with the only solution.

"Put the doughnut bag over my head," I whispered.

Charlie gently shook the bag. "Dude, there are still two doughnuts in here."

"I don't care. Shove them in your gullet and put the friggin' bag over my head! Please!"

"Then wut?" Charlie asked, mouth now packed full of confectionary delight.

I didn't have time to explain; Blake was just a few yards away. Charlie yanked the bag over my head, showering my freshly washed (and not even slightly straight, thank you, expensive miracle product) hair with crumbs and sugar.

I could hear Blake's footsteps getting closer. Since I couldn't see what was going on, here is a transcript of what I heard:

BLAKE: Hey, Charlie! What's up?

CHARLIE: Oh, wofthin', dwood.

BLAKE: Really jamming on those doughnuts. What are they? Powdered sugar?

CHARLIE: Wep.

Oh, no. All the powdered sugar was making me need to sneeze. I felt it brewing. My eyes started to water. Come on, Charlie, move it along!

BLAKE: (laughs) And up to some early-morning vandalism? Right on, man. Is that statue new? I've never seen it before.

CHARLIE: Mwusta wot it while yoo were away.

BLAKE: True. Just remember, doing stuff like that is what got me in military school in the first place.

CHARLIE: (big gulp) Noted.

I couldn't hold it in anymore. A delicate but audible *achoo!* radiated from my paper bag.

BLAKE: What was that?

CHARLIE: I, uh, had a little sneeze there. That's all. Allergies. Outside. All that.

BLAKE: Bananas!—it sounded like it came from your little stone friend!

CHARLIE: Ah, yes! Ha! How funny and unlikely that would certainly be.

I cringed. Charlie always got super proper when he was nervous.

BLAKE: Uh, okay. See you, man.

CHARLIE: Indeed, sir.

BLAKE: Man.

CHARLIE: Man?

After the sound of Blake's footsteps were out of range, Charlie whipped the bag off my head.

"Oh, dear." Charlie wrinkled his nose at me. "It appears you've been attacked by the Sugar Plum Fairy."

~

"Well," Charlie said, skipping along in sheer annoying merriment, "you are stuck with these powers, right? So why don't we use them to our advantage?"

I sighed, dragging my still-heavy legs down the English department hallway. "I don't have any control over them, remember? I just need to wait for them to go away."

Charlie replied, "This might be permanent."

I stuffed my books in my locker, hoping he was wrong.

"Or, it might not be. It might just be some... puberty thing." I nodded my head, agreeing with myself.

"Puberty?" Charlie laughed. "I'm hoping to come out the other end of that a bit taller and with a sweet goatee. What will it leave you as? A fire-breathing Gollum or something?"

He playfully smacked my shoulder. At this point, I couldn't help but laugh.

"Come on, study hall," Charlie said.

"Not me. I have an appointment with Doctor Dirk."

"Eesh," Charlie commiserated. "What did you do to get slapped with a guidance counselor chat?"

"Nothing," I said searching my memory. "I mean, nothing that he would know about. I hope."

"What if Doctor Dirk figured it out?" Charlie gasped.

"Are we thinking of the same guy?" I joked as we headed separate ways.

Doctor Dirk Phillips was an old-school hippie-type dude who wore velvet vests and once caught his office curtains on fire while burning incense. Hey! We finally had something in common. I wasn't worried he'd put *any* pieces together about me and the fire. In fact, I'd wager the only pieces Doctor D had ever put together were of the jigsaw puzzle variety.

~

I watched the school secretary, Mr. Fenkel, search for his lost car keys and was mildly fascinated by just how many tissue boxes were on his desk. From what I could see, the desk itself may have been made with tissue boxes.

"Miss McGowan?" Mr. Fenkel droned through his cottony white teeth. "You may go in."

I smiled before I opened the door.

"Veronica, I'm your new guidance counselor, Ms. Watson." An angular woman in a stiff navy-blue business suit leaned over her desk and shook my hand.

I felt the corners of my mouth fall. "Where's Doctor Dirk?" I asked. For the first time in my four years at Pearce Middle, I actually missed him.

"Doctor Phillips was reassigned," she said as she sat down. "I thought it would be wise to get some facetime with everyone involved in the event the other day."

I leaned back in my chair. "Me? I'm totally fine. All is well."

"You weren't traumatized?" Ms. Watson leaned in.

My mind raced. Traumatized? How would she know about my trauma? Maybe Charlie was right. I should be paranoid. Suddenly I realized I hadn't talked in a long time.

"The fire? A lot of your classmates are having a hard time dealing with the fire. They feel unsafe," Ms. Watson clarified.

Phew! Just the stupid fire. Not the fact that I had caused it with superpowers of an unknown origin.

I nodded. "Understandable, for sure. It was... scary."

"Why did it scare you, specifically?" she asked intently.

Crap. I needed to get her off the whole fire topic.

"Well, middle school is generally scary. There's no need for a fire to make it scarier... er. I guess."

"You're frightened on a daily basis? What frightens you, Veronica? Do you feel different than the other students? What happens when you get frightened?"

she asked, holding out a cardboard rainbow-colored Emotion Wheel. "Show me on the wheel."

Yikes. Time to diffuse the situation, McGowan.

"Aren't we all supposed to be different? You know, sparkly little stars so special and unique?" I gave a clown-level smile.

"Yes, yes. Sorry about that." Ms. Watson leaned back and put on a relaxed face as she set the Emotion Wheel on the edge of her desk. "You are Rik and Rebecca McGowan's daughter, correct?"

"Uh, yes?"

"We may need to schedule a parent teacher conference at some point," she said.

"My dad, sure, but my mom has been gone a long time," I told her.

"And you do not know her whereabouts?" She raised one eyebrow.

"Nope. Haven't spoken in years. Actually, I don't think I could talk yet the last time I saw her." I smiled, but I could feel a tear welling up in my right eye.

Ms. Watson must have noticed it because she became very flustered and started rifling around in her desk. "Oh, shoot. I know I saw he left some…" she trailed off.

I looked away and let the tear dry. Wacky hormones running amuck. Come to think of it, that Emotion Wheel might come in handy…

Not that I'm big on the whole stealing thing, but this was a little hunk of cardboard. I'd bet she had a zillion of them. I stuffed it in my backpack just as Ms. Watson found what she was searching for. Ooh! She had chocolate!

"Can I take two? Charlie will want one. He's big on eating lately," I said.

"He's the red haired Caucasian male? Approximately five foot three inches?" she asked. "He was with you on the television."

I stopped halfway through the bite of my mini Mounds. "You saw me on the news thingy?"

"Yes, that's why I was particularly interested in talking to you. You seemed so… so affected, I guess."

Now, any normal teenager (aka Charlie) may have totally freaked out at this point. To most it would seem that Ms. Watson was fishing, especially after asking about my parents. Like, maybe, just maybe she knew something about my powers and wanted me to fess up. I wasn't taking the bait, because I knew it wasn't real. This woman had come to counsel, not haul me off to some laboratory. There was absolutely no proof Ms. Watson had anything to do with any organization that might have knowledge of what I could do.

"Well, until next time." I smiled at my overly zealous acquaintance.

"Righty-o!" replied Ms. Watson, not even looking up from her papers.

The door shut behind me. I was chewing the rest of my chocolate, but didn't taste it. I was lost in thought. Where had I just heard someone else use that corny old phrase? Then it dawned on me: the detective who called the other day had said it. Was that a thing people still said or was Ms. Watson the detective? Nah, couldn't have been her, I tried to convince myself. I threw the candy wrapper in the trash, but my arm wasn't moving very fast. I looked down to see several thick, smooth chunks of something on my arm. My hand slid over a light green piece. The stuff was expanding! It looked familiar, like my old turtle, Darby. Ms. Watson had really gotten to me! I was growing a turtle shell!

It was time to employ my favorite old sweatshirt. It may have seen better days, but a few rips were nothing compared to the shiny green shell it was covering. I zipped it all the way up.

As I headed out the door, I was unlucky enough to trip over Betsy, who was on one knee taking pictures of the Eisenhower statue in the front quad.

"McGowan!" she grunted.

"I'm really sorry," I said. All I wanted was to get out of there before anyone noticed how hard and lumpy I was.

"You ruined my shot!" she yelled as she grabbed my shoulder. I tried to wriggle away to avoid the pain, but instead of feeling her vice grip of a hand, I felt... nothing.

All I heard was a soft hollow *thump*. Betsy had grabbed my shell!

In the tussle my sweatshirt had been pulled off one shoulder, and the edge of my shiny green shell was popping out near the hood!

"What the heck?" Betsy retracted her hand and gave me a befuddled, slightly grossed-out look.

113

"Uhhh," I stammered as I pulled my sweatshirt tight around my neck, "I-I've been working out!"

I broke into a run—Mr. Smith should've seen me!— and headed home. I had one more idea for how Charlie and I could get rid of my powers.

But it was gonna get messy.

chapter seven
Emotional Rescue

"It's kinda trippy," Charlie said as he spun the Emotion Wheel I had "borrowed" from Ms. Watson. "What are we doing with it?"

"Well," I said, joining him on the floor, "I was thinking that maybe if I went through *all* the emotions, I could get rid of my powers. You know, purge them. All at once."

"That, my friend, is a very smart idea!" he said.

"Thank you. Listen, Charlie," I said carefully, "this is probably gonna be pretty intense. If you don't want to hang around for it, I totally understand."

"What? No way! I am staying for this freak show."

I gave him a look.

"I mean, I am staying—as your best friend. To support you through this rough time," he quickly corrected himself.

"Uh-huh."

I picked up the Emotion Wheel and pondered where to start.

"How are you feeling now?" Charlie asked. "Maybe we should start on the easiest?"

That seemed logical, for sure, but to figure out how I was actually feeling right now? Man. I was feeling... everything. I was anxious and excited and terrified and annoyed and... hungry.

"Chips," I said, jogging over to the cupboard.

"As much as I truly *feel* that 'chips' is a valid emotion, I can't seem to find it on this wheel," Charlie said. "Do you have anything in a 'happy' or 'confused'?"

We laughed and for a second, everything seemed normal, like it used to be. Just me and Charlie, eating chips in my TV room.

"So, let's get to it, eh?" Charlie pushed, crumbs falling out of his mouth.

The happiness of the moment was definitely broken. Oh yeah, I was a freak.

"Pick an emotion, any emotion," I offered. It was the best I could do in the situation. I wasn't sure how I really felt about anything, let alone what any of those feelings meant.

Charlie closed his eyes and waggled his finger in the air a few times before smashing it down on the wheel.

"I choooooooose you!" he yelled as he opened his eyes.

"Hmm. Grief. That's an interesting one," he said as he tried not to laugh.

"Okay," I said, forcing myself not to smile. "I just need to think of things that I've lost."

I closed my eyes and focused.

Crunch!

"Charlie, that isn't helping."

"Sowwy," he said through a full mouth. "Think about griefy things, please."

"I'm trying." I sighed. "Do you have to keep eating right now?"

"Yes. I'm a growing man," he added, "and I think I'm about to have a growth spurt."

"Are you sure? You may just explode one day."

He hit me with a throw pillow. "How about the loss of your mom?" he asked.

"I didn't 'lose' her, she left," I grumbled.

"Okay, Fancy-Pants Feelings Lady, what about the whole loss of your normalness? Like, you think these powers are the worst and now you're probably stuck with them forever and will never ever ever be the cool and popular person you think you aren't."

Crap. He was right. He was really right. I started to feel the sadness, the feeling of loss, lurking just behind my eyes. It started to sink, heading for my stomach. I was never going to get what I wanted if I couldn't get rid of these powers. It was draining. Like, really draining.

"Holy baloney," Charlie whispered.

"What?" For some reason I also whispered.

"You're slowly turning black and white." He was still whispering.

"Okay, maybe that means it's working?"

"Shhh!" he scolded me.

I tried to focus on my loss, but it was hard. I kept thinking about Charlie shushing me, and then, of course, I heard:

Crunch crunch crunch!

I stifled most of a giggle, but the rest came out as a loud trill. I opened my eyes.

"Ha!" Oh, man, I *was* black and white. I looked like an old cartoon. But now that I was laughing, something even stranger was happening. Every time I laughed, a tiny, cartoony black-and-white bird flew from my mouth and started flying crazily around the TV room. They dive-bombed everything and left splashes of birdy mess—in Technicolor, mind you—all over the beige shag rug.

"No, no, no!" I cried as I took cover under the coffee table. Charlie was faring worse than I was—he held a coaster over his head. It wasn't helping. He was being pelted left and right. Ewww!

"Very!" he shouted, dodging the winged warriors. "You need to get your power back!"

"Get my power back? What are you, a motivational speaker?"

"No, change your emotions and maybe they'll disappear!" Charlie managed before slipping on something lavender and falling on his butt.

Not a bad idea. *All right, Veronica, you are strong, you are powerful*, I told myself over and over and over again. I didn't really feel it, mainly because I was hiding under a coffee table while trying to ignore Charlie's shrieks as he failed to get himself upright.

Okay, being powerful meant being strong. I thought of all the times I had been physically strong—I could carry *all* the groceries into the house in one trip if I wanted to. That was pretty freaking tough. My arms were beginning to feel warm, and they seemed to be slowly puffing out from my body. I was feeling quite powerful, and my muscles seemed to be growing right along with it.

I did it. I actually controlled my powers. I flexed one of my gigantic muscles. So cool!

"Very!" Charlie squealed from behind me.

I turned to look at him. He was still flailing on the ground as little birds pecked at him and pooed all over.

Our floor looked like one of those splattery paintings we saw at the museum.

Wait, it hadn't worked? Suddenly, I felt really helpless. This was a disaster, and I had caused it all with my uncontrollable stupidpowers.

I reached out to him from under the coffee table, but I was stuck. My gigantic arms had wedged me tightly between the table legs. I grabbed a leg with my free hand, and it immediately snapped like a twig between my fingers. The table then toppled over, setting me free.

"Crackers! Who knew that table was so weak?" The instant I grabbed the table, it crumbled in my hand. Was it me? I gingerly picked up a remote with two fingers; batteries and buttons showered from it. I touched a throw pillow with one finger, and the stuffing exploded through the room.

"Charlie!" I yelled, reaching out to him again.

"No!" He crawled away from me. "Don't touch me! You'll accidentally mangle me."

Charlie made it out of the room and shut the door behind him.

"Not that I don't love you dearly," he said from the other side, "but I'm just going to wait right here until things... chill."

I looked around. The room was absolutely trashed. I carefully sat down on the floor, trying not to destroy anything else. I took a couple deep breaths and closed my eyes. I didn't know what to think—except that I needed to stop trying to force these feelings. That was not the best idea I had ever had. For sure. Soon the squawking stopped, and I felt birdy feet on my shoulder. My arms had started to shrink back down.

Now I just needed to clean up this mess before Dad got—

"Yo!" I heard my dad bellow as he came in through the garage. Einstein's nails clicked on the wood floor as they got closer.

"Ugh, hi, Mr. McGowan!"

"It's Rik, Chuck. Where's Very?"

"Um, uh. That's cool you take Einstein to the office with you," Charlie stalled. "He seems more like a work-from-home kinda pup to me."

Popping sounds filled my ears. Apparently, even the dive-bombing birds didn't want to face my dad's wrath. They had destroyed themselves.

The door squeaked open.

"Jebus Pizza, Very. It looks like freakin' Wrestlemania in here!"

Like most benevolent dictators, my dad doled out a swift and fitting punishment. Charlie and I were supplied buckets and cleaner with the promise that he and I would have a "talk" once the room was clean. The only bit of luck on my side was that Dad couldn't ever figure out the remotes, so missing one meant nothing to him. I was fairly sure he wouldn't even notice.

"This is disgusting," I said, squeezing a multicolored sponge into the brown water.

"Smells a bit like candy, though, doesn't it?" Charlie leaned in toward a turquoise splash. "Like blue raspberry."

"Why don't you try it?" I dared him. He ignored me.

"So, what do we do now? What's next?" Charlie asked.

"I don't know. I certainly can't have anything else like this happen. I mean, none of our experiments have been successful, like, at all."

"I wouldn't say that..." Charlie looked around the room. "Maybe just keep cataloging your emotions and their corresponding powers in your sketchbook? Tick them off on the Emotion Wheel? Maybe they will still go away when you hit them all. It was a good idea, Very. Maybe they just need to come naturally."

I reeled. "That's about a zillion emotions. That could take years."

"You're a teenager—hormones will prevail. It'll take about a week, tops," he snickered.

"Hardy-har-har," I didn't laugh.

"Got a better idea?"

I sighed. "The best thing I can do is keep my head down, my mouth shut, and wait for this whole thing to blow over."

Which I guess meant hiding until I was an adult.

~

Once the mess was cleaned and Charlie went home, I tiptoed upstairs to Dad's room and gently knocked on the door. Time for the Dad Inquisition. I had no idea what I was going to say to explain away my stupidpowers; "art project gone awry" was probably my safest bet.

"Dad?" I said as pathetically as possible. He didn't answer, but I could hear him talking inside. He sounded mad, which wasn't unusual if he was on the phone. He hated the phone. This time he sounded angrier than I had ever heard him on the phone. I pressed my ear to the door.

"...well, there is nothing to say because there is nothing going on, okay? Period."

A second later he let out a heavy sigh and swung open the door, leaving me standing there like I had been eavesdropping. Which was a little true.

"Hi," I said sheepishly. "Prisoner McGowan is here for her sentencing."

Dad shook his head. He looked sorta sad. "Just go to bed, Very. It's fine."

Fine? Wait, what? "Is everything okay, Dad?" Now I was worried. No questions, no explanation, no further punishment? This wasn't how Dad acted. Ever.

"Yeah, yeah," he said abruptly and then gave me a big hug. "You cleaned up the mess, don't do it again."

"I won't?" I said as I watched him walk down the stairs. I had never seen my dad so out of sorts and I didn't like it. Whoever he was on the phone with had gotten under his skin.

I scratched my head as I pondered the morality of what I wanted to do now. Dad had left his phone to charge in his room... It wouldn't hurt just a quick look to see who he was talking to. Maybe I could help. I typed in his phone password (it was my birthday, I had programmed it for him) and looked at recent calls. The last entry didn't have a name, just a number. The rest were either me or work or his grey bearded biker buddies. I added the number to my contacts and went to my room. A quick Internet search and I had a lot of results for that phone number, but to get a name or address, I had to pay a fee. With a credit card. Come on! Thus ended my internet sleuthery for the night. I had another day of

127

stupidpowers to contend with tomorrow; I needed some rest.

~

"Veronica!" Derek's smooth voice cut through the chaotic din of everyone fleeing school as fast as possible on a Friday afternoon.

He also startled me something fierce. I wasn't used to hearing anyone except Charlie and teachers shout my name at school. A metal horn with, like the one I used to have on my bike, popped from my head, blaring *Awoooa! Awoooa!* I smacked it into my locker and slammed the door before Derek could see what had happened.

"Alarm on your locker?" he asked, raising one eyebrow.

I tried to look casual and leaned back against the locker. The alarm was trying to escape by bashing itself repeatedly into the door.

"No. Just a crazy ringtone," I managed to make up.

"Do you need to answer it?" Derek asked, mildly concerned. Phones were really important to him.

"Nah... it's probably just..." My mind had gone blank. Did I know anyone? This was taking too long. Just say a name, dummy! "... my mom," I blurted out. I could tell my face betrayed me.

"I see." Derek took a small step back. "Anyway, I just wanted you to know that Keesha can't be on Spring Formal Club now."

"Oh, that's too bad," I said. "What happened?"

Derek furrowed his brow, clearly not sure what to say. "Jenny, um, I mean, *we* decided she needed to go. That's all I can really say."

I nodded like I knew exactly what he meant. I had no idea what he meant. (*Awoooa!*)

"I mean, we were fine without Betsy, but having *two* open spots is just too much extra work, you know?" Derek added, "So, like, you want in?"

"Me?" My attempt at laid-back? Not so good.

"Yeah... um..." He delicately picked through his white messenger bag until he retrieved a smoothed-out, blood-splattered sketch. It was one of my dance ideas!

"We found these and thought, you know, why not? Apparently, you're cool with the work and stuff. So,

129

meeting after school, 'k? At Café Blasé." Derek was already walking away.

"Yes!" I said before I really thought about it. Then a certain *Awoooa!* brought me back to reality. Crap! How could I possibly hide forever if I had life-altering, awesome-making, Est-creating meetings? It didn't really matter. There was no choice. I had to do this. Period.

The only thing harder than having stupidpowers would be convincing Charlie that I should be in the SFC.

~

"That's a rare sight," Charlie said.

"What?" I asked, even though I already knew what he was talking about. I was smiling so hard it was beginning to hurt.

"It looks like your teeth are trying to escape your face. Tell me, what do your shiny human teeth know?" Charlie demanded as we walked.

I started skipping. I have no idea why, but I just went along with it. That's how happy I was.

"I, Veronica McGowan," I started, "am now a member of... *the* SFC!" I stared at Charlie, expectantly.

He shook his head. "No. No no no. That is, like, the anti-lay low plan, Very!"

"Well, yeah, *but* it's also the only thing I have ever wanted, and it's happening to me now. *Now*! How could I possibly refuse?" I gushed.

Charlie slapped his palm to his forehead. "Uh, what?"

Now I was getting irritated. This was *so* Charlie.

I stopped skipping. "Why can't you just be happy for me?" I asked.

"Happy? Happy?" He grabbed his hair, pretending like his head was exploding.

"Yes! That's what friends do. They are happy for each other when good things happen."

"Well, you and I have a rather different definition of friendship," Charlie said. "As your friend, I believe it's my responsibility to look out for you, no matter what. Even if you don't agree, or don't like it, or grow some scary kaiju shell."

"You saw my shell?" I pulled my sweatshirt up tighter around my neck.

Charlie gasped. "You had a shell?"

He was so excited, I couldn't help but laugh and, of course, no longer be annoyed.

"Ah, the magic of friendship!" I waved my arm in the air grandly.

To both of our surprise, a small rainbow arched from my arm.

"Holy cow! I controlled that!"

"You did?" Charlie asked.

I wasn't sure, but I didn't feel *out* of control like I usually did.

"I-I think so. Maybe that means it's almost over."

"For your sake, I hope so," Charlie said, "but for superpowers' sake, I hope it isn't."

I arrived home feeling far more positive than I had in quite some time. Things were finally going my way. And the next stop was everything I had ever wanted!

Well, if I didn't accidentally singe the SFC with my stupidpowers.

chapter eight
Eat Your Greens!

Café Blasé was like a lot of things in our town—new, yet somehow inexplicably dated. Opened by someone who obviously had their glory days back in the mid-1990s, like most of our parents, it was a time capsule dedicated to round furniture, primary colors, and *Friends*. Still, it was the best we had. Our only other option was the local Parkin's Family Diner. There we would, undoubtedly, be given colorable place mats and children's menus. At least Blasé's owner, Frank, had no qualms about selling overly sweetened coffee drinks to kids. Err, young adults.

I had rushed to get my things and plow out of school so I would have a few minutes at home to compose myself and reapply some makeup, which wouldn't do me much good, but made me feel a bit prettier. There was something really satisfying about applying lip gloss even if I couldn't keep it on for longer than half a second. My speediness seemed to pay off. As I got close to the door, I could see there were no other SFC members in the café yet. But there was someone there I really didn't want to see. Not today, at least. Or, more aptly, not until I felt and looked and acted like a totally different person. An awesome, beautiful person who could compose complete sentences.

Blake.

This time I didn't have a doughnut bag over my head, I could actually see him. His hair was different, and better. Didn't hang so much in his eyes. That's a thing. I guess.

Hair.

Boys.

People.

Wait, what was I saying?

I needed not to process any of this on an emotional level. If I could Robot Veronica this whole encounter, which I realized was probably about to happen, I might be okay. Hooray! A respite! The whole SFC had arrived in a single drove. I could just slide on in with them. If Blake even noticed me (unlikely), I would look wildly popular and possibly even normal. Not at all like a girl who spends her evenings being entertained by the King of Pretzelasaurus.

"Veronica. You made it," Jenny said in a more factual than pleased tone.

"Sure did!" I couldn't help but sound overly zealous as I held the door for everyone. "Excited to get working!"

We passed the pastry case in a huddle. I stayed closer to Kate than either of us was comfortable with, but we would have to endure. Blake was sitting only a few steps away at the counter.

"Yuck," Hun Su said under her breath when she spotted him.

I knew the truth, though. I could see a familiar look in her eye. Forbidden fruit, baby. If there were polar opposites in the world, Hun Su and Blake were certainly them. I could see the appeal in dating the "bad boy" whilst also totally irritating one's parents.

Although I realized my own dad would probably be thrilled if I could snag Blake—a man after his own heart.

On second thought, maybe I needed to date an accountant.

Blake turned at exactly the wrong moment. We locked eyes. A half-crooked smile crossed his face. It took a few seconds before I realized I was smiling back like a complete and total idiot.

I was sure that at some point in my life I had known words. Lots of words, even, but at the moment, I could find none. So I just kept walking and sat down with the rest of the SFC and pushed Blake out of my brain as much as possible. I had things to do. This was it! This was the good stuff—the beginning of my new life as an Est. Artiest. I took a few notes in my sketchbook and nodded a lot. Proof that I was completely on board.

The presence of Betsy with a camera couldn't even ruin my high. Besides, she was there to document the SFC, which now included *me*. I would be right in there—smack dab in the center—for the two-page yearbook spread. Although, Betsy was evil enough that she would probably find a way to cut my head off in the pictures. I crouched down so I was at the same height as Hun Su and leaned closer to her. I did my best not to look creepy. At least this way I could ensure my face would make it into the yearbook. Even Betsy wouldn't dream of cutting out Hun Su.

My neck started to get a crick and as I slowly bent it out, I noticed Hun Su wasn't really paying attention to us at all. She was looking off into the distance. I followed her gaze. I shouldn't have. She and Blake were deep into a flirt of epic proportions. Their eyes would lock, then she'd look away, and then he'd look away. Then they'd look back at each other and restart the whole disgusting process.

Hun Su? Really? *Really*?! They weren't from the same planet. She thought he was gross. He thought she was snotty. (Or, at least, I had decided that in my own head.)

Blargh.

I looked back at my sketchbook and filled in my doodle of a puppy. I guess I got it—Hun Su, with her perfectly straight, glistening hair... Then I noticed my hand. It looked a bit sick. As in, really green. No! I was turning green with envy. I had to find a way out of here without anyone noticing. But I couldn't. Pinned between Hun Su and Derek, I was trapped. I picked up one of the oversize menus and began "studying" it intently.

"Ummm, now décor?" Kate asked.

Shoot. That was my cue. I couldn't put down the menu—I was still green. Hopefully no one had noticed my green finger tips peeking out the sides of the menu!

"Veronica? Knock, knock!" Derek pretended to knock on the menu.

"Uh, hi! Yeah. I'm just really hungry," I said.

"You can put the menu down for two sec—Ouch!" Derek ripped his hand away.

I may have smacked it when he tried to pull down the menu. (Okay, I totally did. I didn't mean to. It was a natural reflex.)

"Ha!" I forced a laugh. "Be careful. I bite." Worst. Joke. Ever. *Fix it quick, Veronica!*

"Um, I have a whole stack of sketches right there next to my notebook. Pick what you like!" I said.

"Okay..." Derek trailed off as they flipped through the pages.

"Ooooh! I like this one!" Kate cooed.

"No way, this one is totally better!" Jenny said definitively.

Yay! They liked my ideas. They really liked my ideas. It sounded like they were splitting into two camps. They couldn't agree, and it was getting heated. How cool. My jealousy was fading as the compliments kicked in. My skin was now more celery than a kale.

"Stop it! Let's pick Kate's favorite!" Derek shouted over the din.

"Nooooo!" Hun Su complained.

"Ugh! Stop it, guys." Jenny instantly silenced the rabble. Queen Bee speaks. "Just, like, mix the ideas. We can mix the ideas, right?"

More silence.

Oh, no. She was talking to me. "Yeah! Yeah, sure. I'm sure I can combine them," I said from behind the menu, but really I had no idea.

"Cool," Jenny said. "Everyone done being children now?"

There were embarrassed murmurs of agreement amongst the troops.

She let out a deep sigh. "Okay, let's talk about how I am not dealing with food this year. At all. It is way too stressful, and you all know Hun Su has issues with guacamole."

Kate started talking about possible snack options and educated us on all the food sensitivities that were popular that year. Since the controversial Peanut Ban a few years ago, their options have been a little limited. Do they go vegan? Gluten-free? Do they need to worry about everything being kosher? In the end, cupcake flavors were decided upon (red velvet and carrot cake), and everyone was blissfully happy about a job well done.

More importantly, I looked at my hands—the green had passed, and I could *finally* put down the menu. I realized I hadn't ordered anything, but no one seemed to care. These were *my* people. *My new people* who talked about new things like reality TV shows and some new pop princess and her ancient actor boyfriend I had never heard of. For a brief moment, I felt my attention wane. My brain seemed to have an urge to inform me that all this talk, this "important" talk, was not important at all. I shut it down with a *big* swig of coffee. Which, I discovered, I forgot to put sugar in. Yuck. In the midst of my sour face, I caught a glimpse of Blake leaving. I waited, but he didn't look over his shoulder or anything. I tried to brush it off as no big deal. Sure, we hadn't seen each other in almost a year, and last time we did I thought he was going to kiss me. Boy, was I wrong.

"Veronica, is that cool?" Kate's shrill soprano cut through my daze.

"Uh, yes!" I replied wholeheartedly to whatever she had said. For all I knew, I had just agreed to eat nothing but glass for the next five years.

Jenny smiled. "Excellent. We've never had anyone be spirited enough to take on *both* food and decorations."

My fake smile got bigger and more painful. "Both? So, what will all of you be doing?" I tried to ask calmly.

"I don't know..." Jenny thought for a moment. "Whatever, I guess."

I started organizing the sketches in front of me, finally seeing what two themes they wanted me to combine for the dance decorations.

The first was Equestrian.

Cool, yep, got that. Saddles, hay, funky saddlebag pants. No biggie. You could mix that with anything, right?

How about vampires?

Vampires and horses. In case you missed it, that's what we're talking about, kids: Vampires and horses. For our last spring formal in middle school. I opened my mouth, but nothing came out.

"We're excited to see what you can do, Vanessa. Maybe even make you a permanent member of the SFC, if the dance is a success..." Derek winked at Jenny.

I wasn't sure I was supposed to see that wink. A sadness crept inside me that even the shiny newness of SFC couldn't glaze over. Here I was in my new life, but had I really changed at all? Were they just trying to use me? Good old *Vanessa.* My eyes started to tear up. *Fight it, Veronica!* I pretended to sneeze and wiped my whole face with a napkin. I refused to let myself cry.

"Ahhhh!" Kate cried.

Suddenly, water was pouring on us!

"Sprinklers! Run!" squealed Derek.

With that, the SFC gathered their laptops, designer purses, and smart phones and disappeared. Café Blasé was completely empty. Except for me. I didn't move. I had already looked up and knew there wasn't a sprinkler malfunction. There was a girl malfunction that had manifested in a giant rain cloud directly above my head.

The downpour lasted my entire walk home, contained to a three-foot perimeter around me. I wanted to go inside, but I was in a bit of a pickle. My desire to be horribly depressed in private was impossible without taking the storm with me. The last thing I wanted to do was spend the night sobbing and mopping, trying to clean up all the water before Dad got back from working at the club.

I sat on the front steps and let the rain do its thing— at least my sadness could clean the porch. Wow. That sounded like a bad poem.

All I could really think about was how Charlie and I had failed to fix me. I stretched out and onto my back, thinking it would force the cloud to change position, maybe even throw it off completely, but the cloud stayed put and I got a face full of water.

"Gah!" I leapt up, engulfed with anger.

I grappled at the cloud as a red light gleamed from my eyes. My throat burned. I knew this feeling—it was the same one I had when Besty took over the art contest. I opened my mouth, sending a bolt of fire into the cloud, drying it up instantly.

Finally, I smiled. "Take that, you jerk."

Out of the corner of my eye, I spotted a small envelope that the mailman had stuck under the mat. I wasn't expecting anything, so it was a lovely surprise to see my name on it, typed with what looked like a typewriter. No return address. This was either from someone really cool or someone really old. Possibly both.

I looked into the settling darkness. I felt like someone was watching me, but I couldn't be sure. If there was anything I had learned in the past few days it was that my senses weren't very sensible. Time to go inside. Shower. Tea. Envelope. Logic. I might not have control of my body, but at least I could try to regiment my mind. Heavy emphasis on "try."

Three hours and six minutes later:

Yeah, admittedly, that was a stupid idea.

The package was less of an everyday envelope and more of a life-altering-confusing-rip-out-your-hair-mind-blowing-crazypants envelope. Inside it, I found a newspaper article. It was about a "freak" ice storm that had encapsulated my house twelve years ago. There it was, our little bungalow with its stained-glass windows, completely frozen. Giant icicles hung from the drainpipes, like they do mid-winter when Dad constantly reminds me how often "those suckers kill people." That seemed normal until you looked at the scene that surrounded my house. The people were wearing shorts and sunglasses. Kids were buying ice cream from a nearby truck. I looked at the date again—July? I guess that was the "freak" part of the storm, huh? I was only about six months old in July, which meant my mom was still around. It was bananas to think that we were in that house at that moment when the picture was taken. All three of us together. I couldn't remember what that was like at all.

Sitting at the kitchen table, I flipped the article over again, and examined it for any clue to where it came from. My Calming Chamomile tea had gone cold again, but I didn't care. Apparently my house was the only one in the whole town hit by this random storm. Why hadn't dad ever told me about it? And why would someone send this article to me? Looking around at the trail of wet footprints I'd left after the raincloud incident, it seemed rather obvious—it had something to do with my stupidpowers. Had someone figured it out? I realized the more important question was: *who* sent this?

I knew where to start, and he was pulling into the driveway right now.

chapter nine
Technical Difficulties

"You really should be in bed," Dad yawned as he cracked open a beer.

"Agreed. *But*, what the hell-lliocentric world view is this and why would anyone send it to me and who would that person be?" I burst out as I handed him the envelope and article.

Dad turned the envelope toward the light. "This was on the porch?" he asked.

"Yeah."

"Interesting," he said calmly.

"That's it? That's all you got?" I gawked.

He tucked the article in the envelope before putting it in his back pocket.

"Look, that was a really weird thing that happened years and years ago," he said.

I waited for him to continue.

Spoiler Alert: He didn't.

"And?" I prodded him along.

"And," he paused, "and there were a few people who really latched on to it. You know, conspiracy freaks. Wanted to annoy us all the time."

"Who?" I asked.

"Just people who want to make big deals outta nothin'." He shrugged.

This made absolutely no sense. My dad. The Dad. This man who wanted to know every single little detail of my day *every* day. This man who made safety his job didn't know who these "conspiracy freaks" were?

He chuckled at my befuddled look. "What?"

"So, I shouldn't be concerned about this? Like, a crazy person sending me an old clipping isn't something I should worry about?"

He shifted in his chair, which creaked loudly. "It doesn't mean they are crazy. Or dangerous. Just means they want to start this garbage up all over again. Don't feed the fire, Very. Nothing is wrong."

Phew! For a second there I was worried that there was actually really something to worry about. More than the things I was *already* worried about. Then he opened his mouth again.

"So, has anyone approached you?"

Great. "You mean, like someone with a hacksaw and crazy eyes?" I asked.

"Very..." he groaned.

"Dad..." I groaned right back at him. "Why are you being so mysterious?"

"I'm not. *You* are being dramatic." He snickered.

That was the most ridiculous, insane, stupid, repugnant, irrational thing I had ever heard. (And, no, I don't actually know what "repugnant" means, but it sounded appropriately foul.)

"Listen," he said as he took my hand in his, "I know that if anything weird or scary happened that you would tell me. Just like you told me about this, right?"

Oh, geez. He was guilt-tripping me and didn't even know it. "Right."

"We're all we got, so let's take care of each other. Which means not listening to nut jobs and telling each other the truth."

I nodded in agreement while guilt gnawed at my heart. It was true; my dad was all I had, and I was all he had. That was the biggest reason to keep my powers a secret. (Other than eternal humiliation, I mean.) If anyone found out, who knew what would happen to me and our little family?

Dad smooched me on the head as he headed to the living room. "You're so much like me it's ridiculous. Also, a bit annoying."

"Oh, shush, you giant booger."

"Love you, kiddo!" he added before clicking on the TV.

Well, freaking wonderful. That conversation left me even more confused. Could Dad have possibly seen my stupidpowers? Nah, that wasn't like him. If he had seen anything he would have said something, right? *Yep,*

Veronica, he would have said something. Just like you did when you got your powers...

~

The next day I was eager to tell Charlie about the newest mystery weirdo in my life, so I invited him over to do some research about the article.

"So, who do you think sent it?" Charlie asked after I'd laid it all out.

"My dad thinks it's conspiracy nuts, and maybe it is... but maybe it's her," I felt my cheeks warm up.

"Do you even know where your mom is?" Charlie asked.

I shook my head. "But what if it *is* her, Charlie? What if she has these powers, too, and she's trying to reach out? I mean, it makes sense, right? Maybe that's why she went away."

"Whoa," Charlie chuckled, "that would be rad, but why wouldn't she just stop by for tea or something? You two could boil the water with your powers."

"I don't know—" I stopped short as I scanned the search results for the article. No matter what we typed in, we couldn't find any record of that freak storm, let alone the article.

"It's like it was wiped out of our own history," Charlie said questioningly. "Are you sure it happened?"

"Yeah, even Dad says it did. I don't understand why something this big wouldn't be anywhere on the Internet when I can easily find the precise lineage of my dog for the past hundred years!"

"Conspiracy!" Charlie thrust his arms in the air like he had just made a goal.

More and more, I was beginning to wonder if he was right.

~

I had spent the rest of the weekend getting ideas together for the SFC to approve. The dance was only two weeks (?!) away. It was time to push into high gear. Charlie had stuck around and helped/mocked the entire process. At least he agreed that their theme was problematic. Unfortunately, on Monday he had a much bigger problem waiting for me before lunch.

"Slow down, Charlie!" I said as I tried to understand the garble coming out of his mouth. He was talking at a million miles an hour, but in a whisper. Really, who is going to understand that?

"I-I was just in the library napping. And so was Betsy. She was uploading her photos there since the art room— She walked away while they were transferring and I—I saw you!" he huffed and puffed.

"Betsy had a picture of me? Whoop-de-doo. She's the class photographer," I said as I grabbed my sparkly blue lunch bag from my locker.

He looked over his shoulder, darting suspicious glances at everyone in the hall before he leaned in closer to me. "You. Were. Green."

Wait. What?

"We gotta delete those pictures, Charlie. Like. Now!" I was already dashing down the hall.

I peeked through the library window. Inside Betsy was hunched over a computer with an angry look on her face. It was hard to tell if that look was because she saw a Jolly Green version of me or if it was just her normal, everyday anger.

"What do we do?" Charlie whispered as he peered over my shoulder.

"I guess we have to distract her. Then delete the pictures. Then run for our lives before she rips our spleens out through our noses," I said.

"That sounds about right," Charlie agreed.

Getting Betsy to move would be easy. And, really, I mean "easy" as in "putting myself in the line of great physical (and probably emotional) harm." There was only one problem.

"If I get freaked out enough, my stupidpowers are going to do something," I reminded Charlie, and myself.

"True. We don't need her to have any more photographic evidence," Charlie pointed out. "I guess that means I'm the bait and you're the switch!"

"But we are just deleting. Not switching," I told him.

Charlie nodded. "Yes, yes. You get the drift, though. You don't have to be so literal all the time."

"Literally?"

heather Nuhfer

"I'm literally going to murder you. Literally," he snarled as he swung his arm in the air, about to pretend stab me.

"Ahh!" I quietly moaned as I put pressure on my fake wounds to stop the flow of pretend blood. I lay "dead" on the linoleum floor while Charlie pretended to kick me. It was one of our best fake death scenes to date.

"Don't be dead!" Charlie whispered frantically as his playful jabs suddenly turned forceful.

"Ouch, dude, that really hurts!" I told him, while keeping myself as dead as possible. "Literally."

"No! Get up, Betsy is coming!" He grabbed my leg and dragged me around the corner and out of sight just as Betsy opened the door.

"Can you keep her away for a few minutes?" I struggled to stand up without making a sound.

"I don't really have a choice, do I?" Charlie asked.

"No. Sorry," I added, "But you are the best ever and I totally appreciate it."

"Just try to not burn the place down." He winked at me before he chased after Betsy.

"Yo, Betsy!"

Betsy had left the photo browser up, and it didn't take long to find the pictures of my stupidpower moment at the café. I thought I had done such a good job hiding behind that menu, but I didn't even think about the giant window behind us. Betsy had gone outside and easily caught several pics of my profile while I was trying to dodge glances from the SFC. I actually looked pretty good in those pictures! My hair was even normal looking. These may have been the best pictures ever taken of me. Well, you know, besides the green skin. I tagged all the pictures and hit the "Trash" icon, even remembering to empty the trash afterward. A hard-learned lesson from the time I had used my webcam to take some glamour shots that were so embarrassing I immediately deleted them. Or, so I thought, until Dad found them and posted them on my bathroom mirror.

Anyway, these less-than-glamour shots were deleted. But I needed to get them off the camera, too. How did I do that? This camera was *way* fancier than anything I had ever used. So many buttons! And what seemed like a zoom feature that could see the surface of the sun! That's why the pictures were so clear and (*sigh*) undeniably of me.

It felt like too much time had passed. Charlie was great at distraction, but not that great.

Yep. I heard Charlie shout, "Hold up, Betsy! I have to tell you something!"

Followed by, "Hey, don't touch me, you freak!"

I flipped through screen after screen of green me, but there were too many to delete them one at a time. I needed them gone, now! I didn't know what else to do—

"Sorry, pretty camera." I flinched as I smashed it to the ground. The lens cap broke off, taking some of the actual lens with it. The back had taken a big bruising, too—a big crack that destroyed the touch screen. I pressed the power button, but nothing happened. I tried one more time for safety's sake, and still nothing. I had officially killed the evidence, and in a few seconds, Betsy would kill me, too.

Very literally.

I set the camera on the ground and artfully arranged its mangled pieces. There. It just fell. It really just fell and broke. Gravity, man. What a jerk. Yep. Yep yep yep. It was time to get out of here.

"What are you doing, McGowan?" Betsy yelled as she thundered toward me.

I stood and held my hands up in the universal "It wasn't me!" position.

"I, uh, I think your camera fell, Betsy. I'm sorry."

"Fell?" She scrambled to pick up the pieces and cradled them like a baby. In an instant her eyes flickered from sorrow to murder, and she looked directly at me. "You did this."

"What? Me? Nooooo." I backed away from her.

Charlie stuck his head in the room and saw Betsy's rage. "Uh-oh. I think we need an adult." He looked down the hall. "Any adult but that one! Very, we need to jam. Now."

"I saw you. I saw! And you don't want anyone to know!" Betsy screamed as she grabbed my arm.

"Ow! I don't know what you're talking about," I said, grimacing from her thick fingers cutting off my circulation.

"You're a liar!" Betsy was absolutely irate. (And, admittedly, right.)

"What is going on in here?" Ms. Watson called from the doorway. She held the top loop of Charlie's backpack—with Charlie in it—so he couldn't get away. "Unhand her! This instant!"

"She smashed my camera, Ms. Watson!" Betsy showed her the wreckage.

"The *school's* camera," Ms. Watson corrected.

"No, she bloody well didn't!" Charlie sounded really convincing, too, mainly because he thought he was right. He had been outside the room when I'd sent the camera to the sweet, photogenic hereafter.

"Yes, she *did*. I know it!" Betsy was really starting to lose it. "That little freak wanted to get rid of the evidence!"

She finally let me go and pushed me towards Ms. Watson and Charlie.

Ms. Watson raised an eyebrow. "The 'evidence'?"

Betsy threw her hands up in the air, ready to slap down some justice.

"She. Was. Green," Betsy said proudly.

"Green?" Ms. Watson looked at me.

I didn't know what to do. I kept my mouth shut and rubbed my throbbing arm.

"Charlie! Veronica!" Ms. Watson motioned for us to follow her. It was time to leave, and I knew exactly where we were going: straight to Principal Chomers and a million miles from Est-hood.

chapter ten
The Ssssentence

Ms. Watson had decided to make us sweat it out in her office while she and the rest of the office staff sharpened punji sticks for the pit to which we were about to be sentenced. No doubt authority would soon impale us.

"Shall we poke around?" Charlie asked, lifting a paper off her desk.

"No!" I smacked his hand. "Aren't we in enough trouble already?"

"Everything is going to be fine, Very."

"Nuh-uh," I said. "I can't be found out now! I'm so close to becoming an Est. This dance means everything."

"Wait, wait, wait," Charlie marveled. "The dance? *That's* what you're most worried about? Not your magical superpowers?"

"They can wait until after the dance," I said as calmly as I could.

"No. The dance can wait! Est junk can wait!" he proclaimed. "This is getting serious, Very."

"*You* are talking about serious?" I was astounded. "You're the one who has thought this whole mess was awesome. I'm going through with the dance, Charles. My stupidpowers aren't going to stop me."

"Unbelievable..." Charlie muttered.

"What are we talking about in here?" a voice interrupted. Charlie and I jumped.

"Nothing," I said flatly. "Nothing at all."

"Mr. Weathers, Ms. McGowan. What are we to do with you?" Ms. Watson asked when she was finally settled in her chair.

"Let us go home, perhaps?" Charlie asked.

I lowered my head. Ugh. Ms. Watson didn't even crack a smile.

"What happened? And why do I have Betsy swearing that you were green and you destroyed her camera, Ms. McGowan?"

I needed to keep my cool and keep my stupidpowers at bay.

"Well," I sputtered, "I *was* green..."

Charlie's eyes nearly popped out of his head.

"... with envy," I added. "Isn't that how the saying goes?"

Charlie caught on quickly. "Yes! And we went to Betsy to ask her not to use those unflattering pictures of Very."

"B-but by the time we were all together, the camera was already on the ground," I said. Now that I was fibbing, and knew it, I felt a stupidpower flare-up starting. I felt sneaky and slimy, like a snake.

"So why would Betsy randomly blame you for breaking the camera?" Ms. Watson asked.

"Because Betsy *hatessssss* me," I actually hissed. I snapped my mouth closed and looked at Charlie, mentally telling him to take over.

"Uh, yes," Charlie picked up where I left off. "Betsy bullies Veronica on a regular basis. Everyone in school knows that. Hates her guts, some would say."

I nodded in silent, yet total agreement.

"And what was the scenario in which you 'turned green'?" Ms. Watson added air quotes to her question.

I was scared to open my mouth. I needed to mind my Ss.

"I wa—I mean, at Bla—I mean, at... café with... formal club when I got..." Crud. What was an S-less word for "envious"?

Luckily, Ms. Watson interpreted my silence as embarrassment.

"So, you saw the Spring Formal Club? And you were jealous of them?" she asked.

"No. I'm *on* the S-SFC." It was a stutter more than a hiss. The stupidpower was fading as long as I was telling the truth. "I, uh, wasn't jealous of them, I guess."

"What were you jealous of?" Ms. Watson asked in a voice that was oddly soothing.

I could feel Charlie staring at me. Wasn't this humiliating enough? Now I had to fess up to something that would make Charlie tease me for the next bazillion years?

"It wasn't anything, really. There was just someone else there. Can we please not talk about this?" I muttered to the floor.

"I knew it!" Charlie gloated. "Good old Blakey-Boo."

"Charlie!" I barked at him. "You don't understand."

"*I* don't understand?" Charlie snorted. "Pretty sure I'm the *only* one who understands." He nodded knowingly.

I responded with a look that he hopefully interpreted as "Shut up, you King of All Buttheads."

Apparently, he interpreted correctly. And did the opposite by continuing to jabber.

"On the other hand, Ms. Watson," he offered, "Very here knows how to make a spectacular mess of things."

Why? Why would he say that?

"... but I'm not convinced her new friends will help her clean it up," he added.

Rage, at this point, was not a strong enough word for what I was feeling. I knew Charlie was still talking, and that Ms. Watson interjected a few words here and there, but I couldn't hear them. I took a deep breath and pushed it all down. We needed to get out of this, and, as irritated as I was with Charlie, my vengeance was going to have to wait. I needed to ignore him. To not hear anything he was saying. If I couldn't hear him make things worse, then I wouldn't get upset. If I didn't get upset, I (probably) wouldn't have a stupidpower attack in front of Ms. Watson. I needed to block Charlie out. At the moment it was what I wanted more than anything. I looked over at him and his endlessly moving mouth.

"Gah!" I gasped.

I watched the start of a brick wall that was forming between me and Charlie, then back at him, then pointedly at the wall. Charlie stared back at me like I was crazy. Ms. Watson shared the same expression.

"You guys don't see that?" I asked.

"See what, Veronica?" Ms. Watson looked around the room quizzically.

Oh my god. They couldn't see the wall. *They couldn't see the wall!*

"Uh, umm... that really big fly that just zoomed through here. Really big."

Charlie caught on that I had a problem. "Yeah, Very just hates flies. A lot. You were saying, Ms. Watson?"

"Yes. After this discussion, I have chosen *not* to take this up with Principal Chomers."

"Oh, thank heavens," Charlie celebrated. "Is there anything I can do for you?" he carried on. "Do you need a kidney? I have a spare."

"*But*," Ms. Watson continued, ignoring Charlie, "You'll be spending the next two afternoons with me. After school."

(I half expected her to belt out a super villain-esque "Bwah-ha-ha!")

"Detention?" I asked.

"Yes." She stared at me, her eyes narrowed. "That's what they call it."

"Elementary, my dear Watson," Charlie tipped an imaginary hat and puffed on an equally imaginary pipe, "but you seemed to have missed a very important clue. We didn't do anything wrong."

Ms. Watson did not care for Charlie's Sherlock Holmes impression. "I don't know who did what and I get the feeling that no one is telling me the truth... on more than one account. Therefore, your punishment will be similar," she grunted.

A heavy sigh from Charlie made Ms. Watson frown.

"Do you have a better place to be? Some other activity you'd like to tell me about?" she prodded.

"No," Charlie pouted.

I had a question. "So, what about Betsy? Isn't she in trouble, too?"

"She physically accosted Veronica. There will be a punishment, certainly. I can also guarantee she will be removed from Photography Club, but I'll deal with her separately," she nodded. "Happy?"

Charlie and I breathed a sigh of relief. We wouldn't have to face Betsy any time soon. For now, my tried and true tactic for survival (hiding from her) would continue to work.

Until Ms. Watson messed it all up.

"Actually, it might be therapeutic for the three of you to serve your sentence together, now that I think about it." She nodded again, agreeing wholeheartedly with herself.

"Maybe you can work things out. Ensure that we never again have a situation like the one we saw today."

"But—" I sputtered.

"See you back here at three."

And that was all she wrote. Well, I mean, all she said.

"Thank you, Ms. Watson," I said as Charlie and I gathered up our things.

I pulled the door shut behind us. Things were getting too strange from all angles.

"What happened in there?" Charlie asked excitedly. "Did I miss a superpower?"

I could see the wall was still there, lingering between us.

"Nothing. I really did see a fly," I lied.

Charlie looked confused. "Maybe you need some rest."

"I have an SFC meeting during study hall," I said. "I'm already running late."

I edged around him, trying not to look at the bricks.

"See you later?" he asked as he stared at me suspiciously.

"Uh, yeah," I replied, glancing back just long enough to see another brick forming in the wall.

~

"Hi, guys!" I called as I set my backpack down on the bleachers. Being outside for non-gym activities was a treat reserved for the coolest of clubs.

Kate smiled at me, looking up from a thick history book. "Hi, Veronica!"

The rest of the Ests seemed very occupied, nay, obsessed with their phones. To get their attention I knew I'd have to make a big impression, so I came prepared. In one swoop, I whipped out the gigantic binder I had painstakingly put together early that morning. It held all of my ideas for the dance. And there were... a lot. And maybe some glitter glue. Or, maybe, all the glitter glue I owned.

Glitter semantics didn't matter. They were going to freaking lose their beautiful minds when they saw all the work I'd done!

"So, here are my thoughts for decorations," I said, grandly opening the binder and revealing its super glam interior.

There they were, the horses and the vampires and the vampire horses!

"This is, like, really amazing," Derek said in disbelief.

Thanks for the vote of confidence, Derek.

Still, my heart soared. The other Ests nodded in agreement. My happiness was at an all-time high, which instantly made me worry—this would be the exact time that stupidpowers would come out. Happy! Happy? What stupidpowers come from happy? I could feel my toe start to tap and I wasn't making it tap. That's when I noticed that my head was bobbing as if there was some really great music playing. News flash: there wasn't.

I was dancing. Oh my gawd, I was dancing. Uncontrollably. The stupidest of stupidpowers had me moonwalking in front of the SFC.

Stop, Veronica, STOP! I needed to gain control of my limbs. The entire SFC was staring at me.

"Ha!" I pretended to laugh as I busted into some snazzy jazz hands. "These are just examples of dances no one should *ever* do at a dance!"

"Go, Veronica! Go, Veronica!" Titan shouted.

Oh no, not the robot!!

The SFC turned to see what Titan was talking about. They all smiled and laughed as they clapped a beat for me to dance to—except for Jenny, who was far more interested in trying to show everyone pictures of her dress for the dance. Titan joined me. His dance was definitely a joke. It was the same one my dad would bust out occasionally at a wedding. I think it was called the Running Man? Anyway, he hammed it up for a few minutes while my stupidpowers ran their course. In fact, after he did his final hip thrust, I was still going strong, feeling happy and like I was finally part of the group. That happiness was a problem because it meant my powers would keep me dancing indefinitely. It was getting awkward again.

I worked up all my will and pushed down my happy feelings. I pushed 'em down as hard as I possibly could. It felt uncomfortable, like holding my breath, or a tight pair of jeans fresh out of the dryer, but I seemed to be retaining normalcy. Well, as much as I could be considered "normal." Quickly my arms and legs slowed down, and I had control over them again. I couldn't believe that worked!

I would have to keep this up if I wanted my own Est title. Part of me was beginning to wonder if it was worth it. Did I want to be an Est badly enough? Charlie certainly wasn't happy and he was my best friend. I had expected that if they accepted me, it would feel great, but even that little moment happily dancing had turned into me having to hide my feelings yet again. Maybe if I became Artiest I would feel good all the time? Or like I belonged? I wasn't sure, but I couldn't stop now. I had worked so long and hard just to get here that I had to see it through!

By the grace of the gods of Valhalla, there was a distraction.

"I know all of you are having fun, or something, but listen up!" Jenny crowed.

"Dark Rooms announced they are playing a surprise show Friday at the Oil City Thunderdome! We *have* to get tickets," she exclaimed as she waved her phone in the air. "I'll pay whatever it takes."

"It's impossible, man," Titan sighed. His eyes filled with what appeared to be his first-ever taste of sadness. "I already heard it sold out in seconds."

So, what I was about to say would definitely change things, but what was really strange was that, for about fifteen seconds, I hesitated to even say it. I knew this would raise me way up in the eyes of the Ests, but something about it felt... ishy. Despite that ishy feeling, I said it anyway.

"Uhh, guys? What if I could get you into an even more secret, smaller show that Dark Rooms is doing? For free."

In unison their jaws dropped.

"What did you say?" Hun Su asked.

"I, um, well, I know their drummer. You see my dad and his mom are cousins, so he's my second cousin or something? I don't know, really, but sometimes we have Thanksgiving together," I trailed off, having lost my point as I tried to explain myself.

"Oh!" I remembered where I was going with all of that, "and, uh, they are playing a secret show under a different name at Count's on Wednesday."

"Pfft," Jenny said. "That's a twenty-one-and-over club. Even if you are telling the truth, we couldn't get in."

I smiled, despite wanting to crush Jenny in my hands. I felt a knot growing in my stomach, but I could play it cool.

"Maybe we could come to Thanksgiving?" Titan joked.

Everyone laughed.

"That's pretty neat, though, Veronica," Kate added, though I couldn't help but notice that Jenny shot her a look that turned Kate into a puppy with its tail between its legs. Kate immediately looked away from me and went back to her book.

What the heck? Why was Jenny being so mean? "Well, my dad is the bouncer there. I can get him to let us in," I offered.

Aaaaaand they were back.

"OMG! Really, Val?" Derek put his arm around me.

"It's still Veronica—actually. And yeah, we can go, if it's only a few of us."

"Ahhh!" Hun Su lost it as she and Derek jumped up and down.

"You're 100% sure?" Jenny pressed.

"100% sure," I cheered as I flung my hands up, gesticulating wildly...

... as one does when one is lying through her teeth.

CHapter eleven
(NOt SO) SOlitary Confinement

There it was: three o'clock. Our usual time of joy and freedom had become a slow trudge of doom back to Ms. Watson's office. If nothing else, I was glad that the wall between Charlie and me had disappeared.

"Time for a nap," Charlie said as he pushed open the door.

"Library," Mr. Fenkel droned.

"Oh, my favorite napping spot in the entire school," Charlie squealed.

"You have more than one?" I asked.

"But of course," Charlie explained, "And I rank them by quietness, comfortablity, and proximity to a vending machine."

"Where does the library rank?" I asked as we walked up the stairs.

"Third," he continued, "out of thirty-two."

Outside the library, Charlie flung up his hood as he used his body weight to push the door open. "Snoozeroo City, here I come."

But the library did not look like Snoozeroo City or *any* relaxing suburb from Charlie's imagination. Ms. Watson was waiting there and had turned all but four of the chairs up onto the tables just like the janitorial staff did. In one of the chairs a steely-eyed Betsy already sat.

"Come in. Sit," Ms. Watson barked.

Charlie and I sat down next to each other with Charlie across from Betsy.

"Now," Ms. Watson began, sitting next to Betsy, "here is how life goes: you *children* may never agree, you may never like each other—in fact, you may spend the rest of your lives disagreeing—but the truth is that you have to be in the same room together and not cause a scene.

A little respect, a little understanding. That is a basic requirement in life. And that is what we will be doing for the next two days—being in the same room. Without causing a scene. Sure, Betsy might think it's ridiculous how loosey goosey Veronica is. Maybe Veronica thinks Charlie's accent is dumb and made up."

"But it is," Betsy informed her.

"No it's not," she shook her head.

"Hey!" I objected. To what, I wasn't really sure.

"Maybe we should all sit quietly?" Charlie suggested and for once he, Betsy, and I agreed on something.

Ms. Watson had given the impression that our detention was akin to some kind of water torture, sure to break all of us in the end. She was right. Not soon after we were bored out of our skulls and Charlie asked these impossible words:

"I never thought I'd say this, but, can we do some work or something?"

Ms. Watson nodded.

But the instant we pulled out our phones she added, "No phones."

Charlie and I wandered the aisles trying to find any books that might help us learn about the mystery article. By agreeing to do that, it seemed to help us get along easier while also passing the time. Too bad we both came out empty-handed.

"Nothing here either," he said, standing in front of the cookbook section. "I looked *really* hard."

"You can't just make a newspaper vanish into thin air," I whispered.

"Most of your kind aren't smart enough to use the microfiche machine. Prolly some pictures and junk there," Betsy's voice grumbled from the next aisle.

The microfiche reader! I hadn't even thought of that old, dusty contraption.

"Micro fish? I'm so confused. Did Betsy just help us?" Charlie pondered.

"I think she did?" I wasn't sure. "Let's just enjoy this moment."

Forty-five minutes later:

"It's useless, Very." Charlie covered his eyes. He was completely exasperated.

I had been trying to get the dang machine to work with zero luck whatsoever.

My frustration had mounted to a dangerous level. I tried to calm down while I unplugged the machine yet again. Of course, the opposite happened and a massive static shock stupidpowers shot out of my fingers and into the machine. Whoa, it worked.

"Bah-bah-bah-BAH!" I sang as I flipped the switch on the microfiche reader. It clicked alive, and a bright light shone behind the screen. I was really proud of myself. Sure, I wouldn't tell anyone that the secret to my antique machine success was the result of stupidpowers, but it was success nonetheless. I kicked the power cord out of sight. Hopefully no one noticed that the machine wasn't even plugged in. It was completely powered by me!

Expecting praise from Charlie (at least) I looked around. Instead I saw all three of them laughing.

"What?" I asked.

"It's a good look for you, really!" Charlie chortled.

Lo and behold, once we figured out how to find the film we needed, we found the same article that was sent to me.

"Whoa, Very, look at this," Charlie quietly said as he leaned in to get a better look at the screen.

He had found an article about a freak storm about sixty miles north that looked far too similar to the one that engulfed my house in the mystery article that had been sent to me. That storm hit almost a week after ours. The article also made reference to another storm that had happened a few days before that in a nearby town.

"What is this, Charlie?"

"Add another check mark to the Government Cover Up Conspiracy!" Charlie said excitedly.

Another fifteen minutes of looking resulted in many more "freak" storms in even more surrounding towns. Just as it was getting really interesting, Ms. Watson called time on detention. The janitor was waiting to lock up the library.

Guess our sleuthing would have to wait until the next day. I also had something else that needed taken care of the next day, and it involved convincing a very large man that a few small teenagers wouldn't cause any trouble.

~

"You're outta your noodle, Very," Dad chuckled as he shook his head. "Letting Charlie in every once in a while is one thing—a thing I probably shouldn't be doing in the first place, mind you—but letting in a bunch of your new friends? Nah-ah. Sorry."

He crammed half a cheese Danish in his mouth and took a big slug of coffee before he went back to pretending to read an article about ear candling in *Yoga Today*.

Our Parkin's Family Diner waiter refilled Dad's mug and looked like he was going to ask us if we needed anything else. Then he spotted my intense stare and cheerfully said, "I'll check on you two in a minute...."

I was prepared for Dad's reaction. I knew there was no way he would ever okay the Ests coming to the club. At least, not right off the bat. He would take some major convincing, but I was willing to do the hard work if it meant I came out with an Est title of my own.

I sipped my juice, never averting my gaze. I knew he could feel me watching him and his feigned interest in yoga could only hold out for so long.

I could wait.

I had a lot of patience.

As long as this was all resolved by 9 P.M. tomorrow.

"Come on, Daddy!" I begged. Oh, darn. That was too sappy.

"Un-uh. Don't 'Daddy' me." He smirked, tossing the magazine back into the pile on the windowsill. "This isn't open for debate. Those kids get caught, I lose my job, probably *both* jobs, then we lose our house, and we starve to death in the cold. No more delicious fresh Danishes or waffles with gunk on them for us." He pointed at my choco-banana-peanut butter waffle. "I mean, what would the PTA say if I let you stay out that late on a school night?"

I didn't think it would be *this* hard. There weren't many topics that weren't open for debate in our house, aside from which Beatle is the best Beatle. (Don't listen to my dad, it's totally John.)

"No one will even notice them. It'll be like they aren't even there, I swear. Besides, it can't be *that* big of a deal."

Dad raised his eyebrows. "You realize that letting them in would be breaking the law, right?"

"But you let Charlie in." Dad's reasoning on this was stupid. Stupid, I say. (Just not out loud.)

Dad leaned in and lowered his voice. "I let Charlie in because he is *one* person. A person we trust; not some random kids you barely know. Trust is everything, Very."

"I know, I know..." I mumbled. "But just this once—"

"Zip it. I'm not saying it again." He gave me the look that meant I really really needed to.

I didn't. "Gah! I'm *so* close to being an Est! You treat me like a baby!"

With that, Dad got up and headed toward the door.

"Dad!" I cried after him.

"Hey, grown-up," he called back, pulling a cigar from his pocket as he stepped outside, "thanks for breakfast."

What? And with that, the dude left me with the bill.

After my allowance and all the change had been cleared from the bottom of my purse, I managed to pay the bill and leave our waiter a $0.78 tip. I bet he loved that. In fact, I could imagine he quit his job and went on a lovely trip around the world with that kind of cash. Hopefully he wouldn't be my waiter next time I came in because I was sure he'd spit in my food. Rightfully so.

The walk to school was long, and I knew Dad thought it would give me time to think, time to be reasonable and all that garbage, but what it really did was give me time to get more irritated. My dad was a rule-breaker for most of his life. A big flibbin' rule-breaker. But never when it came to me. He was as bad as Charlie sometimes. In fact, he and Charlie could watch the show together, since Charlie was so cool and everything.

Grumble grumble grumble. Chill out, lady.

By the time detention rolled around that day I had managed to accept the fact that Dad wasn't going to change his mind, and I would have to break the news to the Ests before they showed up at the club the next night. I was not looking forward to that. Even less than I was looking forward to being stuck in the library.

"Here we are again," sighed Ms. Watson. She looked so gloomy sitting behind the librarian's desk. She didn't look as crisp and stern as usual. A fresh issue of a tabloid magazine was open in front of her.

"What did we learn yesterday? Respect?" she gawked as she turned a page in the magazine. "Is respect even real?"

Oh, no. Was she going to be all philosophical like yesterday?

"You can try and try and try, but it doesn't mean that anyone will take your efforts seriously. Or back you up and work for justice. Some people want the status quo over truth!" She looked at us like we knew what she was talking about and should also be outraged.

The *chut-chut* of an automatic camera shutter made Ms. Watson wince. "Enjoying the new camera, Betsy?"

Sure enough, Betsy had a camera, but I wouldn't call it new. It was huge and bits of it were held on by duct tape. The lens cover dangled by a twist tie.

Betsy grunted an acknowledgement.

"Good. Can I speak with you for a moment?"

Strange to hear Ms. Watson sound so... caring? Human?

Nonetheless, Charlie and I used their little meet-up as an excuse to slip away and get back to our article research. On one of the tables nestled way back by the encyclopedias we stretched out a state map and marked every place there had been a freak storm or other weird incident. It was pretty crazy—they formed a trail that followed right along the highway for about one hundred miles north. The last storm had been in a tiny town I had heard of, but never been to, called Westchester.

"Why did they stop there?" Charlie wondered aloud.

"Well, if my mom has stupidpowers, maybe that's where she went? Maybe that's where she is."

"Or maybe it is just some kook trying to stir things up like your dad said." Charlie shrugged.

There was only one way to find out if my suspicions were true, but that would cause some major issues with my dad and now certainly wasn't the time. Charlie and I put the map away and went to rejoin Betsy and Ms. Watson to wait out the last hour of our detention, but Betsy was in the process of leaving with an elderly woman in a faded plaid dress and a crumpled felt hat.

"What the heck?" Charlie asked Ms. Watson. "Why does she get to leave early?"

Ms. Watson sighed. "Betsy is leaving for an appointment at the request of her legal guardian."

Legal guardian? I recognized the woman—it was Betsy's grandmother. She had gotten her dentures from my dad. I had heard Betsy's parents had split up last summer, but I didn't know she had been sent to live with her grandma. Suddenly Betsy's transition from Est to Bulldozer made more sense. For once I actually felt bad for her.

"Not that it matters," Ms. Watson went on after they left. "You two are dismissed."

"Woo-hoo!" Charlie threw his backpack on and raced for the door. He did a little dance of happiness to pass the time while I got my stuff together.

I stopped at Ms. Watson's desk. She was mindlessly drawing mustaches and monocles on celebrities in her tabloid.

"That's a great look for Sandra Bullock," I offered.

"What? Oh, yeah. Enjoy your evening, Ms. McGowan."

"Ms. Watson," I asked, "did you give Betsy that camera?"

Ms. Watson nodded. "Affirmative."

"That was nice of you."

She furrowed her brow. "I just saw a situation that needed to be rectified. 'Nice' has nothing to do with it."

"Well, I'm sure your help made a big difference to Betsy."

"Really?" She sounded amazed.

"Yeah... Teenagers have a lot of problems. I think most of us need someone to 'rectify' things."

She nodded her head slowly like this was the first time she had ever thought about it.

"I mean, that's why you became a guidance counselor, right? To make a difference?"

"Oh, yes! Yes, indeed," Ms. Watson paused for a moment and the look in her eye was suddenly far away, like she was deep in thought. Then she started to slowly nod her head, like she was realizing something for the first time. "Guidance counselors can really change lives and help ignored and belittled voices be heard." Her eyes sparkled now and she actually smiled as she quickly added, "Teenage voices, I mean. Not adult ones."

"Very!" Charlie called from the door. He had put his enormous headphones on and was getting impatient.

"Right," I smiled at Ms. Watson, who, much to my surprise, smiled back.

~

Down in the gym the art contest was being set up and would be up until the dance next weekend. Charlie had to split, but I stayed to take a look. I easily spotted Betsy's *two* entries and felt my newly found empathy for her melting away. One was a photograph of an abandoned shoe in an intersection and the other was a drawing of the same picture. Really clever and original. They were also really good, but don't tell anyone I said that. Believe me, Betsy already knew.

"Where's your stuff?"

I turned to see Blake.

"Hi, uh, what are you doing here?"

"Just meeting some people," he answered.

"They still let you in here?" I joked. I was quite proud of myself for actually making a joke.

"I know, right?" He laughed. "So? Art?"

"Oh! Well, I don't have anything in the contest this year."

"That's a bummer. Art is your thing, right?" he asked, searching his memory.

"Yeah, I was just too late entering."

He nodded as if this was something that happened to him every single day of his life.

I didn't know what to say, so there was an awkward silence. At least on my part.

"We'll see you tomorrow?" he asked. "Jenny told me about the show. Really cool."

You mean the show that I need to tell everyone they can't go to?

"You're coming?" I croaked.

"If that's alright..."

"Yeah, of course!" I gushed. "See you tomorrow night."

"Rad," he said as he left, waving over his shoulder.

Well, there ya had it. My dad had left me no other option: I had to totally disobey him.

chapter twelve
Mission: Incomprehensible

Getting Derek, Hun Su, Jenny, Titan, and Blake in the club wouldn't be too hard if I timed everything exactly, completely, without fail, 100% perfectly. I could do that, right? It wasn't like I had some weird condition that made me randomly have very noticeable outbursts.

Wah-wah.

The plan was fairly simple.

All I had to do was get them through that broken side door and sneak up the stairs into the rafters. No one would ever know. As long as no one saw us.

That was Plan A. I didn't have a Plan B, but I soon learned B stands for "You would B stupid not to have a Plan B."

Derek and Titan arrived at our meeting spot (around the back corner of the club) about fifteen minutes late. I had spent that fifteen minutes biting my nails and holding in about a year's worth of anxiety. So far, no stupidpowers had appeared, which was a relief. A painful, need-to-be-constantly-vigilant-and-not-show-your-feelings relief, but a relief nonetheless.

"You guys know where Hun Su is? Or Jenny?"

"Yeah, they're on their way," Derek said after checking his texts. "Jenny loves to make people wait."

"Hey, B-man!" Titan hollered over my shoulder.

"Shh!" My dad was just around the corner at the front door. Wait, did he say "B-man"? I turned to see Blake coming toward us. He was wearing ripped jeans and a super old, threadbare Mickey Mouse T-shirt. Really, I couldn't think of anyone else who could pull that off.

"Are we ready or what?" Hun Su's voice trilled behind me. Just then, Blake reached us.

"OMG! Blake!" Hun Su exclaimed in a voice that one would normally save for winning the lottery.

What could possibly be causing this moment of epic, unbridled happiness?

Hun Su was wearing an adorable Minnie Mouse T-shirt. Ooof. Did I mention it was tight? Like, really tight? I looked down at my own purple shirt with its crocheted hem. And saw my sneakers. Unlike the other Est girls, there was barely anything blocking my view of my feet. Or filling out my T-shirt.

Blake gave a sly chuckle. "Great minds...What's the plan, McGowan?"

Was it just a coincidence?

"We'll just need to be really quiet. There's a spot where we can hang out and no one will see us. It might be a little cramped with six people, but we'll manage."

"What about Kate and her brothers?" Derek asked as he pointed to the three people who were walking toward us.

"Nine people including me..." I whispered as I did my best not to panic. We were doomed. The spot in the rafters was too small.

Blake leaned into me. "Come on, Veronica, a little mischief never hurt anyone."

For that, I happily silenced the alarms going off in my head and waved the others on to follow me quietly. The club was full, and the opening band had already started their set. It was perfect timing. The room was dark, and this far-off corner was the last place anyone was looking. Except one dude, who regularly had to hide back here.

"Holy crap on a cracker. Very, what is going on?" Charlie asked as I sent the Ests, Kate's brothers and Blake up the steps to the little loft.

"They're just gonna watch the show. No biggie," I said. Once my "guests" had made it up the stairs, I added, "Please don't tell my dad."

"I won't." Charlie crossed his heart.

Above us the Ests had crammed onto the little landing in the loft between the rafters. They were having fun, obviously, as giggles drifted down to us.

"Not much room up there for you," Charlie noted.

"It's okay. There were a few more people than I expected. I'm just glad they made it up without being caught."

Charlie and I sat behind a stack of chairs and listened as Dark Rooms started up. I was so nervous about getting caught, it took all of my concentration just to keep my stupidpowers at bay.

"Where do you think missing socks go?" he pondered. "Do you think they are stolen out of dryers by elves or something?"

"Probably," I said even though I was completely distracted. I smelled cigar smoke. Dad was nearby.

"Are ya sure? I'm holding out for aliens."

I said something, but had no idea what. I was looking between the stacked chairs, trying to spot my dad. There he was, outside the window just below the loft. He didn't usually smoke there! Crudbuckets. If he looked up, he would easily see all the Ests! At least the music was loud enough that he shouldn't hear them.

"Veronica?" Blake whispered. He had crawled down from the loft.

I gestured for him to follow me into the corner (and away from Charlie).

"What's up?" It was hard to find words.

"I just wanted to say thanks for this from all of us. I know it probably isn't easy with your pops," he said. The Ests were waving at me from the rafters. I couldn't help but notice that Jenny was the only one not joining in.

I laughed and went to say more, but there was something wrong with my tongue. I swooshed it around in my mouth. Was it in a knot? A nod would have to suffice. I mindlessly fiddled with a large power cord that was plugged into an outlet strip hung on the wall. I traced the edge of the cord with my finger and hoped I looked coy and not snotty.

"Seriously. Thanks," Blake said as he touched my hand. *He touched my hand.*

I felt this intense electricity between us. It was magical. It was amazing. It was an actual surge of electricity that went through my hand and into the power strip and fried the entire circuit breaker. Instantly the lights all went out.

BOOM! There went the transformer outside. *Aaaaand* all the power for all the homes within a five-block radius.

"Ahhhh!" a shrill cry filled the club. I knew exactly where it had come from: me.

~

They got the generators on pretty quickly. Too quickly, in fact. I only had half of my guests out the door by the time my dad, flashlight in hand, spotted them. Even worse was that all the commotion had gotten the club's owner, Mr. G, out of his office and he had also seen the giggling teen exodus.

"Get back here!" Dad yelled after them as he ran to the door. I hadn't had time to get out and was hiding behind the chairs.

I heard Titan say, "Isn't that our dentist?" as they fled into the night.

"Stupid kids..." Dad muttered as he turned back toward my hiding place.

"And what the heck do you think you're doing, missy?" he called. "Outside! Now!"

I leaned against the bricks and prayed for a quick, painless death as he puffed on his cigar. He had made me

weirdest

wait out there forever while he talked to his boss, which wasn't a good sign.

"So you're saying you weren't with them? And you can't tell me who they are?" he scoffed.

"Nope," I replied.

"This is not cool, Very." He pointed at me. "Don't lie."

Charlie wandered out of the broken side door and seemed to immediately regret this decision.

"Oh, dear," Charlie said to himself, trying not to make eye contact with my dad.

"Who were those kids, Charlie?" Dad asked, still looking at me.

I stared Charlie down. *Do. Not. Tell.*

Dad was getting impatient. "Someone has to tell me or Veronica is grounded. Indefinitely."

"It was Derek and Jenny and Hun Su and Titan and Blake. Oh, and Kate and her brothers!" Charlie offered them up instantly.

"That's all I needed to know. Veronica, wait in the car. Go home Charlie," Dad growled as he put out his cigar and went back inside.

"Charlie!" I screeched, smacking him on the shoulder.

"What was I supposed to do? I'm not going to let you get in trouble for them. You should have given them up, Very," he said. "I heard your dad talking to Mr. G. He wanted to fire your dad. If the cops had found them, the club would've been closed. He had to beg to keep his job."

"Why are you on his side?" I asked. Charlie was supposed to be my friend and support *me*. This was what I wanted. I knew it was a crappy situation for Dad, but in the end no one had gotten hurt. Why couldn't Charlie see that?

And there it was, back again: the wall. It had more bricks now. So many that it was getting hard to see Charlie, even though he could still see me.

"I better get in the car," I said as I looked at the ground.

"Very?" Charlie called after me as I walked away.

~

To say that the car ride had started off a little tense would be like saying you sometimes wear clothes to school. A total understatement of something that would change your life forever.

I was smart enough to keep my mouth shut. The fewer words I said the less incriminating evidence there would be.

Dad broke the silence. "So, what's with you lately?"

Talk about broad questions.

"Nothing," I said.

"*That* was nothing? Very. Tell me the truth."

"Dad, why did mom go away?" I asked. If he wanted truth from me, I needed some from him. If mom had stupidpowers and he knew it, I needed to know.

"You want to talk about this now?"

"Yeah." I was scared enough of what his answer might be that a chunk of my hair was turning white. I could see the whiteness slowly glide down a few strands that hung over my shoulder.

"We didn't agree on how to raise you," he said matter-of-factly.

That wasn't scary. The color seeped back into my hair. "But, that's pretty much all parents, right?"

"It is most parents, but it was different with us." Dad took a deep breath before he went on. "You're not a baby any more so I'm going to tell you something, but it's also going to be the end of the discussion."

"But why?" My interest had been piqued by about a zillion degrees.

"Just agree that you are gonna leave it alone."

"Okay, okay. Just tell me!"

"I didn't feel like you were safe with your mom around," he blurted out like the words hurt his tongue.

Safe? That was really all the confirmation I needed, right? Mom had stupidpowers.

"But—" I started.

"Shush," Dad demanded. "I said that was all I wanted to talk about it tonight and that's all I'm talking about it tonight."

"One question—" I begged.

"No. You were a jerk tonight, kid. I don't owe you anything. In fact, for this stunt, your summer is going to be spent working reception at the dental office."

We said nothing else the rest of the drive. Did Dad know *I* had stupidpowers? It didn't seem like he did, especially if he thought Mom was dangerous because of hers. How could I ever tell him? Wouldn't he think I was dangerous, too?

chapter thirteen
In Your Bedroom No One Can Hear You Scream

Once safely in my bedroom, I flung myself onto my bed and screamed into my pillow, but that wasn't enough for my stupidpowers, oh no. Suddenly I couldn't hear my own scream anymore. I lifted my head and let out a yell, but no noise came out of my mouth.

Woo! Woo! Woo! Woo! a car alarm wailed outside, interrupting my screech-fest. Then another, and another, and another. I looked out the window and saw that every single car on the entire street had its alarm going off.

Whoa. A few remote clicks later, and all the owners had stopped the noise and the flashing lights.

Back to it, I screamed again. I felt the air whipping through my lungs and throat, but still no audible scream.

"Bree! Breeeee! Ooh ooh ooh ooh!" echoed from downstairs. The house alarm?

An annoyed "Goddamnit" from Dad assured me that it was just the security system going awry, not burglars. "Piece o' crap," he added as he typed in the secret code with a series of beeps.

Okay, one more shot at this whole screaming thing. Bracing myself, I screamed using as much force as I could, but no sound came out. None. I kept going, trying harder and harder. Off went the car alarms again, then the house alarm joined in as the front window in my room cracked. Out of breath, I stopped my silent scream. Then I noticed Einstein, who was pawing at his ears, like he does when he hears a high-pitched whistle. Holy cow. He could hear my scream. I had gone supersonic.

"Son of a—!"

It was a noisy night, for sure. My octave-smashing range had not only tripped all the house and car alarms on the block, but also had somehow set a loop in our own security system, which caused it to go off randomly all night. Which in turn, made my dad go off in swearing binges all night. Super fun, guys.

By morning I was exhausted in numerous ways. Obviously, the no-sleep thing was a component, but I also felt wary. And weary. And some other word that sounds like those words that also means emotionally tired. If that word exists, I was too tired to think of it right then. The dance was a mere nine days away, my mom was dangerous, my dad was furious and I was a big old mess of confused emotions. As I walked to school, my phone rang, completely startling me.

"Gah!" was my version of "hello" for that day.

"Tell me that wasn't you?" Charlie dared me to lie.

"How'd you know?" I asked, whispering into my phone.

He chuckled. "Well, something totally bizarre and loud happened in our little town where nothing bizarre or loud ever happens unless it is directly related to you or your house. Deductive reasoning, my friend!"

"Yeah." I sighed.

"Did you mark it in your sketchbook?" he asked.

I hadn't. I didn't really want to, either. It had gotten depressing to look in there and see all the stupid things I had done, even if they were uncontrollable.

While I walked to our usual meeting spot, I caught him up on my "dangerous" mom situation. I was relieved when it confused him as much as it confused me.

"Charlie, I can see you. You're, like, half a block away." I started to hang up my phone.

"No no no!" he shouted. "Just hold up for like fifteen more seconds!"

Purely to mess with him, I slowly went to hang up my phone. Inch by inch, my finger got closer to the "end" button. Charlie broke into a run. He made it just in time.

"Wooo!" he shouted, completely out of breath. "That *gasp* was *gasp* impressive, was it *gasp* not?" He bent over and rested his hands on his thighs. "I think I'm gonna throw up."

"No you're not," I said, and offered him my hand to help straighten him up. If I had any energy left in me, I probably would have laughed. "Come on, we're gonna be late."

"Yeesh, lady. You look awful. What is it?"

"I'm fine," I replied as I closed my eyes.

Of course, I wasn't fine, but lying about how I felt was a habit now. It just seemed easier for everyone involved.

"Yep. You are totally fine," Charlie said. "Obviously."

Opening my eyes, I saw what he meant: there were now hundreds of red, blue, and yellow balls bouncing on the ground. The kind of balls I'd seen a juggler use at the last county fair.

Charlie looked at me questioningly.

Trying to make a path, I kicked a few of the balls. Until I spotted her. Oh, no.

I tapped Charlie, trying to keep my voice down. "Betsy is over there behind that tree."

He pretended to tie his shoe until he found her giant boxy head. "I think she definitely saw that."

"Everything's starting to spin...." I said.

"Well, the world is constantly spinning, Very," Charlie reminded me as he stuffed as many of the balls in his backpack as he could. Then, for Betsy's benefit, he yelled, "Shoddy workmanship here! This backpack was guaranteed to hold three hundred plastic balls!"

Betsy slowly walked away, checking the photos on her camera. Whether she believed those balls came from Charlie's backpack or not was irrelevant at this point. I had a death grip on a nearby stop sign. The spinning had gotten worse.

"You can't go to school like this, Very," Charlie said with actual seriousness. "You're a ticking time bomb. Like, that is an actual possibility with you now. Blowing up."

He was right. I needed to keep my stupidpowers in check and out of sight as much as possible. But where would I go all day? I felt awful, but I couldn't hide out at home. Dad usually came back for lunch and, after last night's shenanigans, if he caught me skipping I'd be toast!

Then I had a thought that I knew I'd go through with, even though my gut told me it was a bad idea.

"Maybe I'll take the bus out to Westchester?" I shrugged not sure if I wanted Charlie to agree with me or not.

"You can't do that by yourself, Very. Actually, I'm not certain you should go at all."

"I kinda have to, right?"

Charlie nodded. "I guess I would want to. But I'm coming with you."

"What about Ms. Watson? She'll be all over us if we both miss school today."

"Ugh. Good point."

"I'll go by myself. It will be alright," I reassured him even though I had no idea if it would.

I was off to see my mom for the first time in twelve years. She had run away. She probably had crazypants stupidpowers. What could possibly go wrong?

~

The bus ride was long, but it gave me some time to catch up on the sleep I'd missed the night before. The other side of that was I had absolutely no idea what to do once I got to Westchester. Probably could've used that bus time a bit more efficiently, huh?

I had brought one picture of my mom from the box back home. Showing it to the local barista didn't help, so I asked a bank teller, a garbage man and a dog walker. By mid afternoon, I felt out of options. No one recognized her. Either she was a hermit or she didn't actually live here. The bus would be coming back soon and I needed to give up.

This was a crazy idea from the start. I bought a soda and went to sketch in the park near the bus station.

I started to sketch a woman in the park who was reading a book. She had the reddest hair I had ever seen—even redder than Charlie's—and a tired face. About three-quarters of the way through sketching, I found myself in the middle of a very familiar cowlick. I held the sketch away from my face. It couldn't be. Here in black and white, I could see her. This woman looked like an older, box hair dye version of my mom!

How could I be sure, though? What kind of weirdo goes up to a stranger and asks, "Hey, are you my mom?" I decided to give into a suspicion that had been lurking in my belly for quite some time. Opening my phone, I found the contact I had pilfered from Dad's phone. My fingers shook as I pressed the "call" button.

Within seconds, Red was digging through her fringed handbag.

"Hello?" she said. I could see her say the word.

Truth be told, I completely froze. I said nothing, I didn't move, I just watched her.

"Who is this?" she snipped. She waited a beat before she said, "Go to hell" and hung up.

"Moms," a familiar grunty voice complained behind me.

Something in me still wasn't working right, so I was aware of Betsy being there, but my brain didn't seem to process it with the usual amount of fear.

I managed to sqeak out, "Why are you here?"

"The plan was to catch even more of your freak show antics so I can ruin your life," she told me as she sat down.

"Oh," I said, trying to wrap my mind around everything that had just happened (but failing miserably).

"You didn't do anything since you got here, so it was kinda a waste of time. I got far better shots of all your weirdness back home," she said, scrolling through pictures on her new/old camera before she popped out its memory card and put it in her pocket for safe keeping. "Well, I'm sure finding your mom and all that was important, but not to me."

"How'd you know that was my mom?" I was finally making sense of things.

"You both have that stupid hair flip."

219

The bus arrived, and Betsy and I got on it. She sat behind me and gave my seat a good kick.

I decided to ask her something I had been wondering about. "Hey, Betsy?"

"What?"

"Can I ask you a question?"

"I think you probably will even if I say no," she gruffed.

She wasn't wrong. "So, you've seen my..."

"Freakishness?"

"You've seen what I can do."

"And? Wasn't there supposed to be a question in there?" She sighed.

"You don't have any questions? Or, like, concerns?" I asked.

"Nope," she confirmed as she gave my seat another kick.

For some inexplicable reason, it made me feel better.

There was a long pause before Betsy said, "Actually, I think your mom and my mom would hit it off. Does she like rum?"

chapter fourteen
The New Girl(s)

I had timed my arrival back home like a pro school skipper. Not too shabby for my first time. Dad had already gone back to work after lunch, which was perfect because I desperately needed to lie down. Trying to find my mom had just made me feel worse and more confused. All these things, whether it was Esthood or fixing my powers, were just getting harder and less likely to happen. I hated feeling so helpless and small. There were so many things I wanted to be, but not a single one of them was the mess I saw in the mirror. Why couldn't I just be Artiest already? *Why*?

My head spun. I sat on the edge of my desk and waited for it to pass. Einstein had wandered into the room and was making a bed out of this morning's towel and a sweatshirt. Happy as a clam, he picked up the towel in his mouth and rearranged the mass until it was a mangled, uncomfortable-looking pile and then plopped his fuzzy body down like it was the fluffiest cloud in the sky. I joined him and rested my warm cheek on the wood floor. The cold felt good. I was so tired. Tired? Was I tired? A weird giggle popped out of my mouth. Did I just giggle? It sounded nothing like me. My stomach was really queasy. Was I going to throw up? I couldn't tell. Without warning, my arm swung out and smacked against the leg of my desk. Ow! Wait, did that hurt? Was I angry? My brain was in such a fog that I couldn't tell down from up. Maybe I just needed to close my eyes. Just for a second...

When I opened my eyes the first thing I noticed was that I was back sitting on the edge of my desk. Hadn't I been on the floor with Einstein? Maybe I had just imagined that. My head was now cool to the touch, but my face was wet, like I'd been crying.

I went to look in the mirror. Other than the tear-streaked face, I looked normal. No stupidpowers poking out. Something felt off, though. *Really* off. I had this urge to get my sketchbook, but I wasn't sure why. I didn't have anything in particular that I wanted to draw. I reached into my backpack, and that's when I saw what was wrong. My hand, my arm— I looked back into the mirror to see my side view.

I was crazy thin! Not like supermodel thin, but flat, like a cartoon character that had been smooshed by a steamroller. Suddenly, my hands twitched and I couldn't control them. Without any sort of rational thought, I sat down and my hand started sketching. It was like my hand had a mind of its own! With lightning speed, it drew Keesha and me. Or, at least, it kinda looked like me.

My other hand whipped the page over and started on a clean sheet of paper. Again, I was drawing me, but this time with Hun Su at the mall, and I was a beautiful, airbrushed version of myself.

A really sporty version of me.

Again, my hand flipped to a new page and started to draw. It looked like the AP physics lab. I was at the board writing calculations while Kate looked on, completely astounded. As she congratulated me, my hand drifted to the side of the paper to add something to the scene. It was Charlie, peeking into the classroom.

"Oh-oh-ah-ah!" The monkey ringtone signaled that Charlie was calling. My hands still wouldn't obey me, but I managed to hit the accept button with my toe, then mashed at the screen with it until I hit the speaker button.

"H-how are you doing that?" he replied. He sounded totally freaked out.

"Waddya mean?"

"I am looking at you right now and you aren't talking on a phone!" He sounded like he was yelling through gritted teeth.

I whipped my head around and scanned the windows. Where was he? "I'm on speaker, dude. Chill out!"

"How? Why are you at school?" he continued. "And why are you wearing glasses?"

Suddenly it all made sense. Wonderful, awful, horrible, brilliant, awful (did I already say that?), awful sense. The reason I was flat, the reason I was watching all these scenes play out—I had split into three more people. Three more versions of myself. The most epic stupidpower of stupidpowers. I must've still had some kind of bond with those versions of me that made me sketch out what was actually happening. Whoa.

"Very?" Charlie said. I had been quiet too long.

My hand was gearing up for another sketch. With a fresh page and frantic pencil I went for it. This was something big. I could feel it.

"It—that's not me, Charlie. I'm at home. Stupidpowers!" was all I could muster before I accidentally hit the "end" button with my foot.

I could have died a happy pancake of a girl, but it got better. For realz. Cool Veronica just smiled all kinds of casual. I/She was so cool.

Back in my actual house, my old friends—my first stupidpower, the Cutesy Hearts—had filled my entire room, yet again. This time, they were gigantic. I felt woozy. My guess was that there wasn't much left of me to create these manifestations. A look at my hand proved me right; I was now so paper thin that I was almost transparent. I had to hold on for a few more seconds so I could draw what Cool Veronica said. What was her "I wish I thought of that!" answer?

I was drifting out of consciousness when Charlie came bursting into the room.

"Very!" He ran toward me.

My hands slammed the sketchbook shut, popping all the Cutesy hearts in the room.

"What? What what?" I heard myself say as I tried to pull my focus back to reality.

Charlie poked at my arm. "You're plumping up."

I could use my limbs again. I turned to the mirror. My profile confirmed it. I was being re-inflated.

Charlie flipped through my sketchbook. "So, there were drawings of alternate selves in here? Like the one I saw?"

"Yeah, that really happened."

"There isn't anything like that in here." Charlie said, flipping through the pages. All of my alternate-self sketches were gone; they must have disappeared when I slammed the sketchbook shut. I didn't know if that meant all my little Alties had disappeared as well.

"Hopefully that smart one stuck around, and she can take your finals for you."

"Charlie, that's a brilliant idea."

"What the what?" Charlie stared at me like I was crazy.

"I could be anything I wanted, Charlie. Heck, all I have to do—"

"Is let your alternate selves live your life for you while you hide in here like a piece of stained glass?"

"Yes!" It was so simple.

"You've lost it, chica. If you're being serious, then it's time to get some professional help. You realize that, right?"

"Oh, Charlie, you're blowing this way out of proportion."

"Me? *I'm* blowing things out of proportion? You're okay with having the most split personalities ever in the history of the universe, and *I'm* the one with the problems? Ha!"

"Hey, that's not fair. I didn't ask for this to happen to me. Besides, what do you know about problems?" I tried to control my anger as my voice went up a few octaves.

"Problems aren't the SFC or Blakey freaking wakey or you being so stupid you can't even like yourself, Very!" he shouted.

Stupid? That was it. I shouted right back at him. "You don't care that you're an outcast! You don't care that no one likes you or that you don't belong anywhere!"

For a brief, shining moment I regretted what I had said.

"Well, you're right," he said. "I don't care that I'm not an Est, because you know what? Those people are idiots. Mindless little robot people."

I shook my head at him and bit my tongue. There were lots of things I wanted to say, but I didn't want any more stupidpowers today. It had gotten a lot easier just to suppress my emotions instead of feeling them. Suppress for success! (I should get that on a T-shirt.)

Out of nowhere, the brick wall was back, smack-dab between Charlie and me. As usual he didn't seem to see it, but there were far more bricks now, and only a small opening—the size of one brick—was left.

Charlie added, "And now you're one of them."

"Get out," I said.

"My pleasure!" I couldn't see how upset he was, but I could hear it as he stomped toward the door.

"You know, I don't know what makes me feel dumber, the fact that I never noticed how shallow you are or the fact that all this time I thought we were best friends." He paused, then said, "Since we were little kids I've known where I belong, Veronica, and that I only needed one person to like me."

"Ugh!" I threw my sketchbook at the brick wall, but it bounced back and smacked me right in my stupid face.

chapter fifteen
Makeup or Breakup

The dance was less than a week away, and boy, was there a lot of work to do. And I mean *a lot*. I was back to being normal-sized and hadn't seen (or drawn) any of my Alties, so they must have disappeared. It was a relief, but also scary. All of my Alties had really made great impressions on the other Ests, not to mention Blake. Impressions I had to keep up.

Even though it was Sunday, I was headed to the gym to start the banner when Hun Su texted me. She wanted me to come over to her house. Decorations could wait.

Hun Su greeted me at the door of her house that was just as adorable as she was; a pale blue cottage that even had a white picket fence. She had a completely bare face that, not surprisingly, still looked beautiful and poreless.

"You can do my makeup today, right?" she asked hopefully as she led me to her room.

Oh, funk. My Pretty Altie was a makeup expert. Regular Veronica, definitely not.

It was then that she noticed I didn't look nearly as good today.

"You look really tired," she said, then added, "Didn't you have time for makeup today?"

"I-uh, I'm really busy getting the dance stuff ready," I explained.

"I totally understand," she acknowledged. "Could you just do my face really quickly? Please? We're going to audition the final bands for the dance today and I want to look hot."

"I don't know…"

"Pretty please, Veronica? I'll love you forever!" She giggled.

What I should have done is made a better excuse, put my foot down or even faked a sudden and severe illness, but instead I deciced to try. I had watched tons of tutorials online. It looked *so* easy!

Hun Su had all of her makeup organized in a panda-shaped box (cute, right?) and had set up a chair in front of her full-length mirror as our salon. A swipe of conecealor, a dash of lipstick and some eyeshadow. I could handle those... kinda. Then there's they eyeliner aspect of the whole beauty world. Or, as I like to call it, The Eye Gouger.

"Let's get to it!"

The foundation went on a more smeary than I thought it would. I wasn't allowed to use foundation yet, so my skillz were more like skills. Just getting an even layer on her face used a lot of makeup. It looked pretty thick so I decided to add extra blush to give her face more dimension. Contouring, I think it's called. Eyeshadow: aces. Now. Eyeliner. I was super cautious when I started tracing around her eye. Maybe too cautious. When I stepped back to see how the right eye had gone, it was painfully obvious that I was afraid of poking her in the eye—the liner was really far away from her eye! Like I had just drawn a circle around it.

"How's it looking? Cute?" She asked, bubbling over with anticipation. She tried to sneak a peek in the mirror, but I blocked her view.

"Uh, yeah! Cutest thing evahhh," I lied. I totally lied. Lying liar liar. "Ummm," I thought as I spoke, "what do you think about a smoky eye? It would be really grownup!"

"Yes!" Hun Su squealed. She was getting giddy.

A smoky eye was the best thing I could think of, then I could just fill in the space between the liner and her lashes.

"Oh, Veronica!" she gasped. "You should *totally* do our makeup for the dance!"

Oh, boy. "Um, yeah... Maybe." I mumbled as I worked.

"Are you bringing that Russian kid from school?"

Russian kid? "Oh! You mean Charlie. He's British. Not Russian. Well, actually, he's not even British."

"He's cute... in an interesting way." She opened her eyes wide for me to put mascara on her. "But it might be time for an upgrade! At least it's a group date so you won't be stuck alone with him all night."

Group date? Blake didn't mention a group date.

Hun Su's phone buzzed. "It's Jenny. Let's send her a selfie."

"Not yet, not yet," I begged. I still needed to fix this mess.

"Ooh, drama!" She winked at me. "I'll just text her back and let her know we are busy getting pretty."

Her phone buzzed again almost immediately.

"What did Jenny say?" I was hopeful she was warming up to yours truly.

"Nothing." Hun Su grinned, but she didn't look that happy.

Her phone buzzed a few more times, causing Hun Su to sigh deeply before she set it face down on the floor.

"Sooooo, let me see," she playfully demanded as she grabbed my arm.

I stepped back to look at the finished product. *Gulp.*

Hun Su stared into the mirror. "I, uh..."

Again, she put on a fake smile and picked her phone back up. This time her feigned happiness was much more muted. She was trying to be polite.

"Thanks, Veronica," she nodded as she unceremoniously started herding me toward the door. Were there tears in her eyes? The makeup wasn't *that* bad! Okay, maybe it was.

On the way to the front door, Hun Su was texting wildly.

"Everything okay? Are you happy with the makeup?" I heard myself ask even though I knew the answer.

"Um, yeah," Hun Su eeked out.

I tried to lighten things up. "Talking to Jenny? Anything going on? Did she buy another goldplated phone case or something?"

"It's nothing," she repeated as she replied to another text. "Don't worry about it," she added.

"Text me?" I asked as I stepped out the door.

"See you later." Hun Su waved to me off as she closed the door.

After that disaster, I decided to walk up to school and get to work on the decorations. I was much better with a paint brush than a blush brush.

Halfway up the school's long driveway, I spotted Keesha on the track field. I hadn't really talked to her since she'd been kicked out of the SFC, if you don't count my magnificent mile Altie, that is.

"Hey, you!" She beamed at me as she tightened up her sneakers.

"Hey!" I said, sitting down next to her on the grass.

"No sitting, Speed Racer. Let's talk 'n run!" She hopped up, definitely expecting me to follow her.

Halfway around the track, I was just about dead.

"Geez, what were you up to last night?" she joked over her shoulder.

"I think it's these shoes. And wearing regular clothes," I panted. "I'm not as aerodynamic! Are you back in the SFC?"

"Um, yeah, I think so!" she said with ease.

"That's cool." I huffed and puffed.

"I heard you've joined us," she said as she ran backwards so she could face me.

I managed an "Uh-huh."

"A word of caution," she offered, "Jenny doesn't really like being second place. She didn't like it when Betsy was getting all those art awards, she didn't like that I was dating a high schooler, and I'm sure she's definitely jealous over how much everyone likes you."

"But what does that matter? She's still Queen Prettiest."

"Believe me, it matters to her. She invited me back an hour after Mark dumped me," Keesha turned around and zoomed away. "She'll never want to share the spotlight!"

I was left in the dust.

Chapter Sixteen
Beauty Sleep

By the end of school on Monday I was feeling really lonely. I had sent Charlie a bajillion messages, but he hadn't responded. Even after I told him it was majorly important. And, honestly, I had noticed the Ests were often too busy to talk or "didn't see me" when I was walking down the hall. Keesha might have been right— jealous Jenny might be trying to keep me down.

I had stayed up late the night before trying to get as much prep work done for the dance as I could, but I had become preoccupied by something else super important, or, actually, I got fixated on whether I should text Blake and try to clarify that we were going to the dance on a regular date, not a "group date," like Hun Su said. I wrote and erased texts for a good part of the night. Finally achieving this exchange:

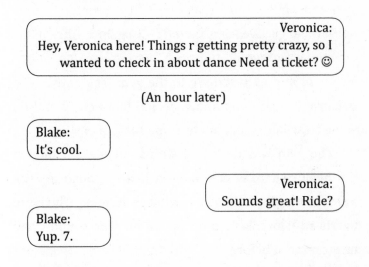

Veronica:
Hey, Veronica here! Things r getting pretty crazy, so I wanted to check in about dance Need a ticket? ☺

(An hour later)

Blake:
It's cool.

Veronica:
Sounds great! Ride?

Blake:
Yup. 7.

And that was it. At least I got a small bit of info from him?

When school was done for the day, I was exhausted. There was so much to be done, though, I had to push through and work on the decorations before I could sleep. I gave the janitor my student ID (complete with horrible photo) and the note from Mrs. Krenshaw that allowed me to be in the school after hours. The dude took his duties seriously as he stared at my ID, then at me, then back at my ID, shining his flashlight in my eyes repeatedly. Did I really look like trouble? I was a half-awake girl wearing a panda sweatshirt. After a few questions that would put the TSA to shame, the janitor let me in and escorted me to the gym. The entire way. Because I might, you know, decide to go crazy and do some after-hours algebra or something. Sheesh.

The gym was dark and strange at night. I flipped the light switch, which made a heavy industrial *click* much louder than the light switches at home. The large overhead lights flashed on with a buzzing sound I had never noticed before.

"Hello?" I said just to make sure I was alone.

Nothing.

I opened the supply closet, which Charlie had helped me to fill with my supplies before he decided he hated me forever. It was packed with what an uninformed stranger might think were the remnants of a Halloween party at a dude ranch.

I slugged all of that crap out of the closet and got to work on the banner. It was a rather mammoth undertaking. Rolled into all the other things I had agreed to do, I had said yes to a banner that read, *"Hay is for horses & Blood is for Vampires!"*

It was one of what I had started to see were *many* poor decisions. That banner would need to be about the length of a whole gym wall!

Just outlining the letters took a few hours and really hurt my knees. I chugged down yet another soda and tried to pump myself up: "Come on, Veronica! This is going to be amazing! You and Blake are going to dance under this banner!" It seemed to work, at least for a bit, and using the wrestling mats to kneel on was a pure genius move, if I do say so myself. About halfway through the coloring phase, I began to really struggle. And by "really struggle" I mean I fell asleep once and face-planted right into some wet paint.

So tired. So very tired...

~

When I woke up, the morning light was hitting me directly in the face. Schnitzel! I bet Dad was freaking out. It was Tuesday morning and I had been at school all night. My phone was dead. I'd have to get my charger from my locker.

Wiping the drool from a wrestling mat, I went to stand up and smacked my head on something. What the what? I was in a bubble. Like, a hard protective bubble. I shook my head, finally waking up fully, and the bubble disappeared. Ah, thanks, Protective Stupidpower Bubble of Sleep and Exhaustion. This was when I also noticed I was in the supply closet. Did I come back in here? I was so tired the night before anything was possible.

I made my way to my locker. No one was at school yet, but they soon would be, and I needed to make myself look like I hadn't slept here. I yawned. Oooof! And I needed to find some mints. ASAP!

Once my phone had a little juice, I expected an onslaught of messages from Dad, but there wasn't anything. I sent him a text telling him I was sorry and explaining that I had fallen asleep in school. His response: *Don't get another detention.* Man, he was still really mad at me.

By the time everyone was at school, I felt like I had done a decent job of disguising my day-old ick. I covered up my top with my trusty old hoodie and still had a knit hat from winter jammed under my overdue library books. I would be hot, considering it was about seventy degrees outside, but at least no one would see my greasy hair. I couldn't believe how greasy it had gotten in just one night! Must've been the stress or something. Bodies. Who understands them?

I spotted Charlie down the hall and smiled at him. He walked right up to me. The wall was gone again. I breathed a little sigh of relief. Maybe he had forgotten about everything or had come around and was going to support me being an Est. I missed that knucklehead.

"Charlie!" I reached out to hug him, but he leaned away. I guess he didn't miss me.

"Did you figure it out yet?" he asked, barely even looking at me.

heather nuhfer

"My stupidpowers?" I whispered. "No. I'm trying to control my emotions now. No more stupidpowers in public, remember?"

Charlie snorted. "Obviously!"

"Charlie, this is stupid. Just. Be. Happy. For. Me. Please. You're my best friend."

He stepped away from me. "You know what? I hope you have a great day, Sleeping Beauty. Really, I should probably call you Sir Snoresalot."

"What?"

"At least I don't have to cover for you anymore," he added before he left.

What did that mean? And why even come over and talk to me if he was just going to give me a hard time? My moment of pondering was almost instantly interrupted by Ms. Watson.

"Veronica!" She waved me over from her office door.

Great. Just what I needed. "Yes?" I asked.

"We need to reschedule the meeting you missed," she said.

"Meeting? The Tuesday one?"

"Indeed," she chided me. "When can you come in?"

"What about tomorrow?" I asked. I'd rather get it done with than have that meeting looming over my head at the dance this weekend.

"Ha. Very cute," Ms. Watson said, dismissing me as she went back into her office.

What a weirdo.

The rest of the day was a lot busier than I imagined. There was even been a history test that I *swore* wasn't supposed to be until Friday. So much for 'All About John Adams'.

My frazzled brain couldn't take much more. I was so happy when the bell rang, even though it meant I had to run immediately to the bloodsucking horses and switch my booty into hyper drive. Getting all the decorations done by Saturday was going to be nearly impossible, but I knew I could do it. I *had* to do it. There really wasn't much of an option at this point; if I didn't get it done, it would be an instant sentence to life in captivity, or, at least, high school at the loser table. Blake told me I was cool. Nothing, let me repeat: *Nothing* was going to funk that up.

~

Waiting for me in the gym was Jenny and the rest of the SFC. I was really happy to see them (and hoped they had come to help) until I saw Jenny's expression.

"What's your deal, Veronica?" Jenny screeched.

"What's up, guys?" I smiled at them weakly. "I know I'm a little behind, but it's cool! Don't worry, the gym will blow your minds when I'm done."

Derek snorted really loudly. "Are you insane? You've done, like, nothing."

"I have it all under control," I said. "There's plenty of time."

"And you think you deserve to be one of us?" Jenny hissed. "You'd better pray for a miracle in the next twenty-four hours, Veronica."

Jenny stomped out of the gym, leaving scuffmarks and a very confused me in her wake. The others followed. Kate gave me an apologetic glance before she left and Keesha whispered, "I told you she couldn't handle it."

Twenty-four hours? What in the all-that's-heavenly did she mean by that? The dance was at 6 p.m. Saturday night, which was exactly... I looked at my phone to get the precise hours and minutes.... Let's see here... today is Friday.

Wait. Stop. Rewind.

It said today was Friday. It still said today was Friday. That couldn't be right. It was Tuesday. I fell asleep in the closet on Monday night....

Then it dawned on me: the horrid bad breath, the hair greasy enough to fry something in, Ms. Watson thinking it was funny I wanted to schedule an appointment tomorrow. My stupidpowers had made me sleep for three days straight. It *was* Friday and the dance was *tomorrow*.

If for a few seconds I hadn't been pissed off at Charlie, I sure was now. When he had told me to have a "great day" earlier, he knew I had been asleep for three days! He frakking *knew* and didn't have the decency to wake me or warn me. Unbelievable.

I was in full panic mode now. Who could I call to help? No one. I mean, really—no one. No one was speaking to me. Not Charlie, not my dad, certainly not the SFC. I couldn't ask Blake to help. How pathetic would that

look? Besides, I wanted him to be wowed by all the work
I had done, too. At school I was pretty much only friends
with Charlie. I really didn't know anyone else. Except...

~

"T'wouldn't be but a finger more forward," Ted said as
he helped me hang the banner early Saturday morning.
He was more than happy to help, or that's what I think
he said. I thought getting Ted past the janitor would be
hard, but it turns out the power of the pretzel compels
us all.

"Hey, Pretzel Man!" the janitor joyfully called out as
Ted shook his hand.

Apparently the janitor filled up a "Pretzelentologist
Frequent Biter Card" every single week over at the
pretzel stand. (For the record, that would be ten pretzels
a week.) Ted had saved my butt by bringing all the
leftover pretzels and many frozen ones to help me fill
the gaps in my food plan. I had baked and chopped
vegetables and smooshed guacamole for most of the

night, but the pretzels would ensure no one would have to dance hungry.

"Hey, Ted," I asked as I climbed down the ladder, "did you ever meet my mom?"

Without hesitation, Ted nodded. "She was a thing."

"Do you think she was dangerous?" My hope was that a simple yes/no question would help this conversation along. "My dad said she was."

Ted scrunched up his face like he was having a hard think about it. "Some folk don't care to like weird."

"But that doesn't mean weird is bad or dangerous."

"Nahz," he agreed. "Weird is wonderful."

It might have been a sign of my impending nervous breakdown, but that sounded really nice. Dad had just decided weird was bad. It didn't mean mom was dangerous. It didn't mean I was dangerous. There was hope.

Just like for this dance! It was really starting to shape up and look like... Equestrian Gothic.

A giddy rush swept through me, and my stupid powers manifested a small fireworks show over my head. Ted was too busy to notice.

"Thanks for the help, Ted!" I high-fived him.

"No cheese, please." He shrugged, then waved away the remaining smoke from over my head. "Bit young for the puff stuff."

"You are an absolute lifesaver," I thanked him again, successfully dodging his remark.

Ted looked at his watch. "Back to it," he said. Then he added, "Besides, you got another one," and pointed toward the back wall. Betsy was helping tear down the art show. I had been asleep so long I had totally forgotten the winners of the art contest had been announced. I could see a blue ribbon hanging from each of her entries. First Place in both categories. Ms. Brannen loved realism, for sure. Betsy caught my eye and smirked, patting her pocket to show me she still had photos of me mid-stupidpower. Great. That was another thing to worry about tonight. Bleh.

I watched Ted shuffle out the gym door, aimlessly searching for his car keys in his oversize pants pockets before I took a moment to look around and appreciate how freaking cool the gym looked. For real. I had taken a few artistic liberties that I was pretty darn proud of.

The mash-up of horses and vampires came together in a Victorian theme with some Dracula-esque touches. Horses with red eyes pulled carriages. I'd spray painted bales of hay black and was serving chips and pretzels in upside-down top hats.

The whole theme was very mysterious, which I thought would play well. Still, I was a little nervous until the big truck of flowers arrived a few hours later. The delivery people loved my decorations. They called them "unique" and "creative." The lady even said that she wished her school dances had been this cool.

My pride instantly took a blow when Jenny and Keesha decided to pop their heads in and see how things were going. Jenny didn't look nearly as impressed as I hoped she would.

"It's alright, I guess." Jenny sighed.

"Are you kidding? It's amazing!" Keesha said before Jenny gave her a death glare.

"I worked really hard on it, so I hope you like it." I genuinely meant that.

"Well, it has my name on it, so I better like it," she sneered.

257

"Excuse me?" I asked. On the other side of the gym I saw Betsy perk up. I'm sure she was loving this.

"I am the leader of the Ests, Veronica. I make or break the SFC and that includes you."

With that, Jenny strutted back out of the gym. Keesha rolled her eyes and followed her.

I looked around to see if anyone other than Betsy had witnessed that exchange, but even Betsy had bolted. I noticed there was still one piece of paper hanging on the wall where the art show had been. On closer inspection, I saw that the paper had been folded in half and pinned up with a tack. "Freak" was scrawled across it. Hmmm. Give ya one guess who left that.

I pried the tack out and as the paper unfolded, a memory card fell to the ground. The piece of paper was a sketch Betsy had done of Green With Envy Veronica. Over the top she had scrawled, "The only people I hate more than you are the Ests."

Considering our past, this felt like a love note. She gave me all the stupidpower pictures. All of her evidence to turn me into a social leper. I took the memory card and put it in my locker. I wouldn't dare take it home and have dad find it. I needed to dispose of it properly, and permanently.

I was finally done. And with two hours to spare. Yikes! I needed to rush home and get ready. At least the chaperones were in charge of getting the food out before the dance, giving me (and my hair) a few extra minutes to primp.

~

Despite the craziness, the sight of my fancy dress made me smile. Sure, it was from Cashman's Outlet, not Chateau Che Whatever, but I thought it was the most beautiful dress I had ever seen. It was navy with sequins and a black tulle overlay. Like a sky full of stars.

Once I was dolled up, I went downstairs. Even if dad was still cranky with me I knew he needed to see this dress.

"Ta-da!" I cheered and did a little twirl as I went into the living room. (I only tripped a little.)

"Yowza! That is a fancy potato sack."

Ooh, Sparkly!

"Thank you, thank you." I bowed as if I had just won an Oscar; gracious, and yet completely full of myself.

"That's why it really sucks to have to tell you that you need to stay home," he said.

I laughed at his funny funny, ridiculous joke.

"I'm serious, Very. I'm sorry, but I'm serious."

"What did I do? Recently?" I added.

"Nothing," he said sadly. "I mean, I let you stay at Charlie's most of the week, right? Kinda evidence that I'm done being mad at you."

"Then why?"

"It's your mom. I think she's gonna try to get you. You need to stay here with me where you'll be safe." He put his hands on my shoulders.

"Safe? Dad, she's not dangerous." My voice shook. I wondered if I should tell him that I went to see her, but decided I shoudn't because: "If you think she's dangerous then I'd hate to see what you thought of me if—"

HONK-HONK!

"My ride is here. I'm going." I turned away, breaking his grip on my shoulders.

"No, Veronica!" he commanded.

I was already out the door.

Chapter Seventeen
Mystery Date

"Hi, guys!" I said as cheerfully as possible as I squeezed in the back seat of the minivan next to Blake.

Kate's oldest brother, Jim, was giving his sister, me, Blake, and Keesha a ride to the dance.

"Hey, Veronica!" Kate said. "That dress is amazing!"

"Oh, thanks!" I said.

"Totally sweet," Blake confirmed.

I was determined to enjoy the night. Sure, Jenny wasn't happy with me, but I had to hope she'd chill out once she had some fun at the dance. I didn't want to step on anyone's toes, but I *did* want to get my Est. Come on, I'd literally torn myself apart dealing with my stupidpowers and working my butt off to get here. Tonight was my night, and no one was going to take it from me.

FYI: I wasn't at all worried about Mom showing up for multiple reasons:

1) How would she recognize me? It had been twelve years.

2) If Dad's big fear was her "dangerous" stupidpowers, I was already well-versed in that crap. She wouldn't come after me to hurt me.

Which leads me to—

3) Stupidpowers do not magically turn you into a goateed villain in a sci-fi movie from the 1990s.

Jim pulled up to school and let us out at the curb. I rifled around in my pockets to find my ticket as we walked up the stairs.

"That dress has pockets?" Blake asked.

"Yes! Deciding factor," I admitted. "I can't do purses, I forget them everywhere."

He smiled and said, "There she is." He was looking at Hun Su, who was giddily waving at him. (Her makeup was flawless, btw.)

"See ya later?" Blake punched me lightly in the shoulder, like I was one of his dude buddies. Then he rushed up the stairs two at a time and straight to Hun Su. They hugged, and then she held onto his arm as they went inside.

What just happened? I stopped on the stairs. Kate patted me on the back as she and Keesha followed them in.

I felt a light mist on my face. *Not now, stupidpowers. Please, not now.* A slight fog had formed over my head threatening rain. Quickly, I waved my hand through it, breaking it up. My heart felt to so fragile and sore. *Veronica McGowan, you're* not *cool.*

The sadness was starting to engulf me. I needed to talk myself out of it before my powers went live.

It was time for a pep talk of epic proportions.

Okay, Very. This is just a little setback. Don't worry about it. Remember when Blake wasn't part of the equation? When getting Artiest was everything you wanted? You can still do that. You can still get that Est! You did the best job ever on crazypants decorations! Own it!

weirdest

The fragile feeling didn't go away completely, but the chances of rain went down by at least 70%. I had this under control.

Until I noticed a bad red dye job was sitting on the top step waiting for me.

"Veronica?" my mom asked, cocking her head to one side and squinting.

"That's me," I answered, but I didn't move any closer to her.

Just like before, seeing mom didn't feel good. Something was missing. What I had wanted was to feel an instant bond, especially since we shared the same stupidpower affliction, but instead I wanted to run in the opposite direction. Or maybe it was just Dad's voice echoing through my head.

"How do you know what I look like?" I asked.

"You know who I am?" She was surprised.

I nodded.

"Well, I saw you on TV," she answered.

How many times did they replay that news report?

She offered me her hand, and I took it.

"You sent me that article, didn't you?" I said. "You wanted me to know about the powers."

"Yes. It was time you knew the truth." She led me down the stairs. "Come with me."

"Did someone cure you?" I asked quietly. My heart was starting to fill with hope.

"Cure me?" She sounded confused. "You are the one who needs to be cured. I don't care what your father says."

I went to pull my hand away, but she was now holding my wrist as tightly as she could.

"Let me go!" I yelled. I could feel my stupidpowers firing up. *Not in public, Very!* I did my best not to process any of my feelings, but I knew I needed to get away from my mom.

"Hey!" Ms. Watson shouted, hurrying toward us from the school. She must have seen what looked like an attempted abduction. (And it sort of was.)

A giant scowl took over Ms. Watson's face when she spotted Mom. "You!"

"Agent Hendriks?" My mom was just as disgusted.

"Agent Hendriks?" I echoed, breaking free from Mom's clutches.

Ms. Watson/Agent Hendriks ushered us behind a pine tree at the bottom of the stairs.

"This woman made our lives a living hell after the first storm, Veronica. Told everyone she could that we were a family of freaks. All for her career," Mom informed me.

"You *are* an FBI agent?" I stared at my guidance counselor in shock.

"A pretty high-ranking one, until your father started filing complaints against me," she said, "then I became one of the most laughed at agents in the bureau. A conspiracy nut."

"So, you came back to prove you were right?" I asked as I sidestepped my mom. "You knew it was me all along?"

"Yes," Ms. Watson added. "Another McGowan in the middle of suspicious activity certainly caught my eye."

"What now? You're going to turn me in? Save your reputation?" I asked. "Mom?"

Mom stepped up. "Well, then you should be really pleased, Hendriks, because that's what I'm here to do, too."

"What?" I shouted, looking for the best escape route.

"You're going to get help, Veronica," Mom demanded.

Again, stupidpowers were raging up, but all of my practice at holding them in was paying off. My brain, on the other hand, was grasping at straws looking for a hero. "Ms. Watson, or whatever your name is, you have to help me," I pleaded. "You're my guidance counselor!"

Ms. Watson stepped between Mom and me. I was sure doom was near.

"You're right," Ms. Watson said confidently. "I *am* your guidance counselor, and I will help you."

Did I just hear her right?

"Veronica, go inside while I deal with your mother."

Holy baloney, I did!

Once I was in the school, my first inclination was to call Charlie. Not too surprising, he continued to ignore me.

"This is Charles Weathers, Esquire. I accept small bills, money orders, and voice mails." *BEEP*

"Charlie, it's, uh, me. Something really weird just happened and... I don't know. I needed to talk to someone, and you were the first person I thought of who would, you know, listen. Um, my mom was here and Watson is totally an FBI agent. Soooo, yeah. Call me. Please."

I hung up my phone and took a few breaths. I had to get myself together before I went into that gym. If I tried my best to be positive, there really wasn't anything worse that could happen tonight, right? Having your crappy abandoner mom decide to send you in for vivisection pretty much tops the Crappy List, so the rest of the night could still be magical. Neigh, it would be! (See, I thought of a horse pun! Things could only go up from here!)

I found the Ests and Blake behind the band's stage waiting to make their grand entrance. I smiled, but they were all giving me funny looks. Kate had covered her mouth with her hands while Keesha comforted her.

A worried Titan approached me. "You should really see a doctor, Veronica."

Before I could ask him what he meant, Jenny linked arms with me and whispered, "I admit, I was kinda worried you'd be hard to take down, since everyone seems to really like you, but it turns out you are lot weirder than I could ever have hoped for."

With that she opened my hand and dropped my locker's padlock in my palm. It had been cut open!

"Your public awaits," she snickered before she shoved me through the curtain and onto the stage.

The goth band stopped playing and someone swung a spotlight on me, causing everyone to turn and look. Some were wide-eyed. Some laughed; some looked downright terrified. What was happening? My eyes adjusted to the lights and I looked behind me. I gasped. Suddenly I couldn't breathe. The projector was not rotating through photos of Victorian England; it was rotating through photos of me with stupidpowers! There I was: surrounded by juggling balls, on the porch with the rain cloud over my head, all of my Alties having a cup of coffee together, and about ten more photos, each more embarrassing than the last.

Then the chanting started:

"Weirdest! Weirdest! Weirdest!"

I wanted to run off the stage, but I couldn't. It was like my legs were stuck. I had no choice but to take the

abuse because, well, I believed it. I was the Weirdest. Every single dream I had was shattered. Every single person I wanted to be thought that I was a freak. What's worse was that they were right.

They were so right.

Nothing could change that now. It was time to let it all out.

chapter eighteen
It's My Party And I'll Destroy It If I Want To

All of the emotions that I had been clenching in? They were about to burst out. There were so many that I couldn't seem to settle on one. The changes from anger to sadness to relief were happening so quickly that the room began to spin. I closed my eyes, feeling my stupidpowers rise up, each fighting the other to be dominant. I didn't have any strength or will left in me to fight them. I was a lost cause and I knew it.

I felt a whoosh of wind and opened my eyes. My stupidpowers had manifested in a swirling, colorful tornado that seemed to contain all of my emotions. There was fire, thunder, lightning, and rain all mixed together. The tornado whipped through the room, destroying everything in its path. Guacamole splattered against the wall; the decorations I had worked so hard on were now singed and flying violently through the air. Everyone ran for cover.

"Yo, Very!"

I turned to see my dad, braving the Veronica-made storm. "Dad? Mom was here! She wanted to take me away!" I shouted at him. I didn't really know why. This certainly didn't seem like a good time to chat, but...

"I know!" He grabbed my hand.

"I hate her! I hate her so much!" I screamed. I couldn't help it. "She did this to me! Then she left us!"

The tornado intensified. The other kids were grabbing onto anything that was bolted down so they wouldn't be swept away. Rain poured and lightning flashed all while the crepe paper and cardboard chandeliers burned.

"She is the reason I'm a freak!" I cried as the tornado ate up everything in sight.

"No, sweetie." My dad grabbed my other hand and pulled me around to face him. "Whatever you are, I was, too."

A crackling noise shot through the gym and I froze. I mean, I *actually froze* everything in the room. The kids, the tornado, the horribly wonderful Goth band, all were completely silent. Everything was encased in a thick sheet of ice, except Dad and me.

"What?" I asked quietly.

"You had them when you were a baby, but they went away. Just like mine eventually did. Just like your Grandma's did and Great Grandma Beatrice's did. I saw the signs that yours were back, but I didn't want to believe it. I didn't want to think about the problems they could cause us."

"And Mom?"

"Your mom threatened to leave and I told her she could never come back." Dad shook his hand like it had fallen asleep. A trail of blue lines on his fingers showed how my iciness had started to seep into him—but he didn't let go of me, despite the fact that he was about to become a real-life Frosty the Snowman.

276

"And you never told me?" I asked. My voice was getting stronger and fiercer as the cold inched its way up his arm.

"She got freaked out after that storm we caused when you were a baby. She wanted to turn us in. She wanted to separate us. I wouldn't let that happen." His voice cracked. "There was an ultimatum. I don't do ultimatums."

"You knew I was messed up. All these years! You *knew*!" I raged on. "And you lied about Mom. You are the one who said we don't keep things from each other!"

His eyes were starting to glisten, but I knew it wasn't from having an icicle arm.

I was glad.

"I just wanted to keep you safe," he insisted.

That's when something inside me broke. That fragile heart cracked and splintered, then fell to the bottom of the darkest pit in my soul. I had given up so much to become an Est. Charlie hated me, and my dad, who I loved and trusted more than any person on earth, had kept this from me, had lied to me all these years. I was alone. And that's how it was going to be from here on out.

I couldn't recover from this. No one would want to be my friend, not even me. I was insignificant, I was worthless, and I *was* the Weirdest.

Or worse, I didn't even exist.

I exhaled as hard as I could, which released a huge shock wave through the gym. It broke up all of the ice, which crackled and shattered as it fell off of everything and everyone. The wave then smashed into the walls with such force that they fell down. All that was left standing was the wall that attached the gym to the rest of the school.

For the first time in a long time, I felt... okay. All of those pent-up emotions were gone, purged from the inside out. Everything was quite literally out in the open, and there was nothing I could do about it. I had to face my stupidpowers. Maybe I was Weirdest, and maybe that was as good as it got.

I mean, really, if I hadn't denied my feelings and let my stupidpowers burst out, the gym might still have all its original pieces.

Oh, snot! Reality check: I just wailed on everyone with my stupidpowers!

Was anyone hurt? I rushed over to Dad, who had been knocked off his feet but looked fine; then I jumped off the stage and began checking on everyone else. My shock wave had hit them, but it seemed like they were all okay. Some were rubbing their eyes like they had just woken up.

I reached down to help Jenny, ready for her to threaten me with lawyers and exile to the front of the bus.

Instead she held out her arm and gladly accepted my hand as she stood. "Holy cow!" she exclaimed. "That was, like, bananas."

"Yeah, I'm sorry," I said. "Things got really out of control."

Titan sauntered over, rubbing his head. "Isn't that the whole point of nature? It's never under control."

"Uh, Titan, I think we need to check you for head trauma," I said, looking for a sign he'd been whacked in the head. Why was he talking about nature?

He gave me a puzzled look. "How do you know my name?"

Oh, crap. His brain must be mush! I made his brain MUSH.

"Here. Sit down," I said, turning a chair right side up. "I'll get my dad to check you out. He knows a thing or two about bodily harm."

I went back to the stage and found Dad sitting on the edge.

"Dad! I think Titan might have a concussion," I said as I motioned for him to follow me. He didn't get up. Instead he just raised an eyebrow at me.

"Dad?" he asked. Then he took a good, long look at me before he shook his head violently as if he was clearing out some cobwebs. "Yeah, Veronica. Veronica. I'm your dad."

We found Titan, who was now surrounded by the Ests.

"Oh, hey, Doctor McGowan," Titan said. "I'm fine. I think that maybe this girl got hit on the head." He pointed at me.

Me?

This girl?

"I'm Veronica. Guys?" They all gave me blank expressions. "I go to school with you? I helped plan this dance?"

"Oh, yeah!" Derek smiled.

"You're in fifth grade or something..." He nodded knowingly.

What in the heck was going on?

Dad gently pulled me aside. "It seems like your little wave of self-loathing made them forget you," he said, giving me a sympathetic look before adding, "but seriously, look at them, maybe it's for the better."

Hun Su was dusting Blake off like a prized antique. Jenny and Derek were fixing Kate's hair, while Keesha stretched and ran in place. I looked at them—I really looked at *them*. Why had I only seen the things they had that I wanted? Every single one of them was terrified of Jenny, they were bossed around constantly. I had enough of that at school. And Jenny. Geez and crackers. I wish her parents' fortune could buy her a surgery to take out her bossy bone. I might not be the prettiest or richest, but I'm also not meanest or scardiest (Let's pretend that's a word) and that was something I could handle. Something I could be proud of.

chapter nineteen
All's Well That Ends Kinda Okay

Dad and I checked on everyone else. One by one, students and chaperones, all confirmed that they had never seen yours truly before. In fact, none of them remembered my powers, what had happened, or me. "Another freak storm" seemed to be the rationale.

"So, why do you remember me, then?" I asked Dad. We could hear the sirens of police cars and fire engines making their way to the school.

"At first I had no clue who you were, but I came around. You are my daughter, ya know."

I hugged him, but my brief flit of joy was snatched away when I spotted a natural redhead motionless under a table.

"No!" I ran to Charlie, and Dad easily lifted the table off of him. "Charlie!" I shouted in his face. "Charlie! Are you okay? What are you doing here?"

I was so relieved to see him, and even more relieved that the stupid wall my stupidpowers had built between us was completely gone. Then I realized the worst thing ever: Charlie wouldn't know who I was. His memory would be wiped clean of me, just like everyone else's.

"He is one tough little dude, isn't he?" Dad remarked as Charlie opened his eyes.

"Well, it keeps me original," he coughed out.

Sure, since he wouldn't know me, the bear hug I gave him might have seemed creepy, but I didn't care. He was okay. I didn't murder my best friend. Err, former best friend.

"I'm sorry. I'm so sorry," I said, letting go of him. "No Stranger Danger, I swear."

Charlie sat up and scratched his head. "I think you would be less of a danger if you were a stranger. I got your message and decided not to hate you anymore. Look at this mess, Very!"

My eyes welled up. "You know who I am?"

"Yeah?" He lifted one eyebrow at me, then looked at my dad. "So, you know everything now?"

Dad nodded. "I think so. Turns out she got them from me. Surprise."

Charlie beamed. "That's the coolest thing ever! You guys need to fight crime or something. Very! How cool is that?"

"You know who I am!" I couldn't get over it. I bounced up and down.

"*Yes!*" Charlie joined me. "Wait. Do other people *not* know who you are?"

"Yeah, that's a stupidpower side effect this time, I guess."

"Then everything is back to normal! No one knows who you are! Yay!" he gleefully danced around.

I couldn't help but laugh. What a butthead. What a wonderful butthead. As usual, he was right. For the first time in a long time, I was happy to be a nobody. In fact, I would take Weirdest forever if it meant I had my dad and my one true friend. I was so happy that a small burst of rainbows flew from my arms as I waved them around. Luckily, by that time, all of the students had been corralled and were busy with the emergency service crews that were giving them clean bills of health.

"Well, if it isn't the old Career Killer," Ms. Watson (I couldn't stop calling her that) said as soon as she laid eyes on Dad.

"Conspiracy nut," Dad growled at her.

"Yeah, obviously." She flung her hands in the air pointing out the destruction.

"Good point," Dad conceded.

"Where's my mom?" I asked her.

"I sent her home, with a very stern warning," Ms. Watson assured me.

"But what if she tells people?"

Ms. Watson snorted. "Who's gonna believe her? I've had a badge for fifteen years and no one ever believed me."

"We don't have to worry about you?" Dad challenged.

She thought about her response for a minute. "Listen," she said. "I'll make a deal with you. I want to stay a guidance counselor, and I'm sure you want to stay off the radar. Let's agree to keep this mystery unsolved and this case file open. Indefinitely."

"Why?" I asked.

Ms. Watson sighed like I was asking her deepest darkest secret. "Okay. Honestly, those paper pushers never appreciated me or my passion for fairness. These kids do. All they want is to be treated fairly and I respect that. I'm staying here."

Without blowing her cover, Ms. Watson was still able to take over the situation (which had now been classified as a mild natural disaster) and keep the cops, reporters, and crazy PTA moms at bay. Once the last siren whooped away, it was actually quite peaceful in the hollowed-out shell of the gym.

"I'll see you two in my office on Monday morning," Ms. Watson said, pointing at Charlie and me as she climbed into her black SUV.

"Hey, I still have a few questions for you, lady," Dad said to Ms. Watson.

"As I do for you, Mr. McGowan."

"It's Rik. Do you have a first name or is that classified?" he teased.

"Ugh. Well, get in the car, meathead, and we'll discuss over pie." She rolled her eyes before shutting the door.

"You okay, kiddo?" Dad asked me. "Wanna go home?"

I shook my head. "Not yet."

"You'll walk her home, Charlieman?"

"Yeah, of course, but I think you've got it backward—I need her protection. It's late! There could be all sorts of weirdos out there. I want to be with the biggest one," Charlie said in all honesty.

"Damn straight," Dad said proudly as he gave me a hug.

He and Ms. Watson took off with a merry little honk good-bye. I was pretty sure the horn played "La Cucaracha." What a freaking bizarro night.

"Well, that was all a bit surreal," I said. "I'm glad I don't have to hide anymore. Well, not from my dad at least."

"Hiding! Wait! Did you see Betsy? She wasn't at the dance! She will remember everything!" Charlie panicked.

I laughed in sheer amazement. "Oddly enough, Betsy is the one person I'm not worried about. I'm not sure if anything could top that."

Charlie grandly bowed and offered me his hand. "We could dance."

heather Nuhfer

"But there isn't any music."

"I know," Charlie took my hand, "and we are in a destroyed gymnasium and you have superpowers. I think we can wing it."

"True," I said as we started to sway.

"Besides," Charlie added, "this is the Spring Formal, and I want to dance with an Est."

Even though my initial inclination was to pinch Charlie hard for that comment (I may have done it, too), he was right. I was an Est. I was Weirdest.

Maybe that wasn't what I had wanted, but it is what I am. And I was starting to believe that wasn't so bad after all.

Weird is wonderful.

acknowledgements

Thank you...

Ashley Eckstein for sharing my dream and making it a reality. Words cannot express how grateful I am for your vision and passion.

Bernadette Baker-Baughman: agent/guardian angel. I'm beyond lucky to have you in my corner.

Tom and Dolly Nuhfer, for their endless enthusiasm and for raising me a proper geek.

Ryan, Crystal, and Logan Nuhfer, Jeremy Nuhfer and Rhonda Schwob and Seamus Nuhfer. I couldn't pick a better, cooler, smarter, faster, stronger, more awesome family than you.

Katie Strickland for being the best best friend and co-conspirator a girl could ever ask for. Thanks for letting me pick your brilliant brain all these years. And for listening to the venting. Oh, so much venting.

Brenda Hickey for her kindness, ridiculous talent, and ability to make sense of my illustration descriptions.

The *Her Universe* crew, especially: Andrea Hein, Dan Madsen, and Cat Carson.

Anthony Ziccardi and Michael L. Wilson at Permuted Press for working so hard to make this book amazing.

Everyone at Victoria Sanders & Associates.

Joe LeFavi for taking a big chance on me all those years ago. You changed my life forever and made it more magical than I ever thought it could be.

Rob Pearce for being the best teacher I ever had and telling me I could be anything I wanted. It meant the world to me.

Mairghread Scott and Erika Lewis for being as kind and generous as they are talented.

Robin Benjamin and Jennifer Brozek for gently cleaning up my wordy messes.

Paul Morrissey for sticking with me all these years. Without your support and encouragement I would have given up long ago. I love you.

about the author

Heather Nuhfer writes all-ages and children's books and graphic novels. She has penned numerous original stories for comic book titles including, *Scooby Doo*, *Wonder Woman*, *Teen Titans GO!*, *Fraggle Rock*, *Lisa Simpson*, and *Monster High*. Her *My Little Pony: Friendship is Magic* graphic novels are international bestsellers. *WeirdEST* is her first prose novel.

When she isn't writing, Heather loves to knit while watching bad 1990s action movies with her beloved furbaby Einstein.

about the illustrator

Brenda Hickey is an illustrator from Prince Edward Island, Canada. She's had an unhealthy obsession with art and comics from a very young age, and can't remember a time when she wasn't drawing. Her most well known work is on IDW's *My Little Pony Friendship is Magic* comic book series.

about
Her Universe Press

Her Universe Press is the publishing imprint of groundbreaking fangirl fashion company, Her Universe. Co-founded by actress and entrepreneur, Ashley Eckstein, and The Araca Group, a leading theatrical production and brand management company. The mission of Her Universe Press is to provide new and aspiring female writers the chance to see their original work professionally published. Focusing on the sci-fi and fantasy genres, the imprint publishes fiction and non-fiction for all age ranges with empowering stories that provide positive messages and a focus on strong female protagonists. Writers, new and established, wishing to submit their ideas and synopses for consideration by Her Universe Press should go to: http://www.heruniversepress.com